Florence Marryat

My Sister the Actress

Vol. I

Florence Marryat

My Sister the Actress
Vol. I

ISBN/EAN: 9783337047177

Printed in Europe, USA, Canada, Australia, Japan

Cover: Foto ©Andreas Hilbeck / pixelio.de

More available books at **www.hansebooks.com**

MY SISTER THE ACTRESS.

A Novel.

BY

FLORENCE MARRYAT

(MRS. FRANCIS LEAN),

AUTHOR OF 'LOVE'S CONFLICT,' ETC., ETC.

' Honour and shame from no condition rise ;
Act well your part : there all the honour lies.'

POPE.

IN THREE VOLUMES.

VOL. I.

LONDON :

F. V. WHITE AND CO.,

SUCCESSORS TO

SAMUEL TINSLEY & CO.,

31, SOUTHAMPTON STREET, STRAND.

1881.

CONTENTS OF VOL. I.

MY SISTER THE ACTRESS.

CHAPTER I.

'WHERE IS MY MOTHER?'

IT is a black, bitter afternoon in December. The snow lies hard and deep upon the ground, its pristine whiteness defiled by the track of wheels and the tramp of multitudinous feet, and the north-east wind catches unwary passengers at the corners of the streets, and stings their faces and makes their ears burn. Through the dingy windows of the London squares, gas-lights may be seen, feebly fighting with the surrounding gloom, and every lamp of the great hall of the Princess College is blazing to enable the visitors assembled to watch the proceedings of the pupils' Christmas examination.

A young girl of sixteen stands upon the platform. Although tall for her age, there is a look of slightness and fragility in her appearance that seems to mock the intellectuality stamped on her broad forehead, and shining in the depths of her dark-grey eyes. She is not pretty, but she is striking. You might mix that girl up amongst a thousand ordinary school-misses, and pick her out as the one most likely to exert an influence over her fellow-creatures. For it is not the handsome women in this world who are the most dangerous. It is those which possess the power of swaying the minds of others.

She has just finished the recitation of a difficult scene from Schiller's 'Joan of Arc,' and the remarkable energy and precision with which she delivered the lines, combined with her knowledge of the German language, call forth a round of applause from her audience. Seldom has the performance of a schoolgirl elicited such admiration. The walls of the college resound with the clapping of hands: two masters, who have been standing by in proud anticipation of the approval that shall reward their efforts on her behalf, leap on the platform to congratulate their pupil on her success: and the soft voice of Miss Denny, the lady superintendent, is heard murmuring her mild congratulations.

But the girl herself seems more disturbed than pleased by the ovation. As the last words drop from her lips, and the applause bursts on her ears, she starts as though suddenly awaking from a dream; she pushes her fair hair impatiently from her brow; her eyes rove wildly over the faces turned towards her, and then, with a hurried but exquisitely graceful obeisance, she fairly runs off the platform. A dozen voices are raised in query as she disappears.

'Who is she, Miss Denny?'

'What is her name?'

'What an extraordinary talent she appears to have!' and 'What a perfect German accent!' being amongst a few of the questions and remarks that the lady superintendent is called upon to answer.

Miss Denny smiles with her head on one side, and coos with contentment, as if the praise were all intended for herself.

She is an extremely self-satisfied, middle-aged lady, whose claims to gentility are chiefly based upon half-closed eyes, a pursed-up mouth, and a voice scarcely ever raised above a whisper. It is so difficult to be vulgar when you never open your mouth. Nothing that is not 'elegant' finds favour with Miss Denny. She is wont to say that 'elegant' is her favourite adjective, and any action, however innocent in itself, that runs counter to the ordinary groove society walks in, shocks her as much as if it were criminal.

'Yes, she is a most promising pupil—

indeed I may say, our *most* promising pupil
—though not always as ready as I could
wish to employ her unquestionable talent in
the right direction,' says Miss Denny, with
folded hands and drooping eyelids. 'Her
name, Lady Harcourt, is Miss Elizabeth
Durant, a daughter of Major Durant of
Northallerton Crescent—perhaps you may
have heard of the family?'

'I think I have,' replies Lady Harcourt,
shortly; and as Miss Denny moves away,
she whispers to the lady next her : 'You
remember my telling you that story about
Major Durant and Mrs. Wallerton?'

'The Irish widow? Is it the same
man?'

'Yes! They live in Northallerton Crescent—not half a mile from here.'

'But he must be quite old to have a
daughter of that age!'

'Not a bit of it, my dear. He's not a
day over forty. Rosa Money says it's a
most miserable household. I have never

seen Mrs. Durant, who is a great invalid ; but I suppose this girl takes after her. She's not a bit like the major !'

'She'll be handsome by-and-by ; don't you think so ?'

'I am not sure,' replies Lady Harcourt, hesitatingly (she is one of those women who never can see beauty in another) ; ' she is very peculiar-looking, there is no doubt : but that fair hair is so apt to lose its colour, and turn out like brown-holland, and clever women are very seldom attractive. They get into such a habit of screwing up their features and looking sharp.'

Meanwhile Miss Denny, who has been asked by several ladies in the company to introduce her talented pupil to them, follows Miss Durant to the antechamber, where the girls who take an active part in the examination are assembled. Here she finds the object of her search, completely indifferent as to what her late audience may be saying of her, but in a state of the most

violent agitation nevertheless, which no ex-
postulations of her companions have been
able to subdue. Her bright hair, which is
the colour of ripe corn at the roots, and
gleams as if the sun shone on it at the tips,
is disordered and untidy ; on her pale cheeks
and the dark lashes of her eyes are trembling
tears, and her thin and unformed hands are
clasped together with what Miss Denny
considers to be inelegant energy.

' My dear Miss Durant !' says the lady
superintendent, reprovingly, ' pray try to
conquer this needless excitement. I have an
honour in store for you. Mrs. Carmichael
and Lady Silver have asked for an introduc-
tion. Just smooth your hair, my dear—I
cannot allow you to present yourself in that
condition, and I will conduct you to the
Hall.'

But the girl she addresses takes no notice
of the request.

' Oh, Miss Denny !' she exclaims
anxiously, ' why is my mother not here ?'

'Your mamma, my dear! I was not aware that she was absent. Are you sure she is not amongst the company?'

'Oh no! no! Do you suppose I should not have known her face amongst a thousand? And'—with a scared look—'I am so afraid she is ill!'

'Come, come, my dear Miss Durant, this is mere fancy on your part! You are over-excited by the success you have obtained this afternoon. Why should your good mamma be ill? Was she not in her usual health when you left her this morning?'

'Yes; but she has suffered so much with her heart this winter. And—and—I don't think anything would have kept her from the College Examination except — except——'

'Miss Ellery, will you have the goodness to step down and ask the housekeeper for a glass of port wine for Miss Durant?' says the practical lady superintendent. 'I cannot permit you to give way like this, my dear,' she continues to Betha Durant, 'you will disfigure yourself terribly ; and Lady Silver and Mrs. Carmichael will be offended if we keep them waiting any longer.'

'*Must* I be introduced to them ?' says the girl, despondently.

'Surely! You ought to consider it a great honour.'

'But I want to go home, Miss Denny ! I want to hear what has detained my mother. Oh, do let me go home !'   ·

'*Go home!*' echoes Miss Denny, with a lady-like little shriek of dismay. 'What, before his lordship the Right Reverend Bishop of the Cockatoo Islands has distributed the elegant prizes ! Miss Durant, I never heard of such insensibility and ingratitude in my life before !'

'And when you are going to get *five* of them, Betha !' whispers her friend and consoler, beautiful Martha Kemyss.

'I don't wish to appear ungrateful,' says Betha, sadly ; 'mother would blame me for that! And I will do exactly as you think best, Miss Denny.'

What Miss Denny thinks best is to order her to smooth her hair and drink her wine, and then to drag her back into the body of the hall, and coo details of her birth and parentage—age, and number of attainments —into the ears of her admirers. Some of the ladies remark her pallor, and ask her if she is unwell, or fatigued by her exertions; and Betha is compelled to pass through the ordeal of answering their questions, whilst her heart and thoughts are far away. At last Miss Denny feels her twitch violently at her arm.

'What is the matter, my dear?'

'There is a lady whom I know—Miss Greene, may I go and speak to her?'

'Certainly, if she is a friend of your mamma's.'

Betha needs no second permission; in a moment she has darted to the side of the lady in question.

' Miss Greene ! have you seen my mother to-day ?'

Miss Greene is so startled by the tone of anxiety in which these words are uttered, that at first she hardly knows whether to say yes or no.

' Oh, Elizabeth ! how are you ? How beautifully you recited that scene, my dear ! I am sure I felt half inclined to cry, though I didn't understand a word you were saying. Your mamma ! Let me see ! Have I ? Oh no ! of course not, but how funny you should have asked me, for I *did* call at the Crescent on my way here, but the maid said your dear mamma couldn't receive me. It is a pity she did not come ! She ought to have been here to listen to your recitations.'

' Oh ! Miss Greene, she was coming—she would have come, I am sure of it, if she had been well enough. She must be ill again. What *shall* I do ? And Miss Denny won't let me go home till the prizes are given.'

'The servant did not say a word about her being ill,' remarks Miss Greene. 'She only said Mrs. Durant couldn't see me, so I thought she was dressing to come to the college. But if she *should* be ill, my dear—there's no need to be frightened — your mamma's so often ill, you know !'

'You don't know—you don't understand,' replies the girl hopelessly, as she moves away. Two more pupils are playing a duet on a couple of pianos by this time, and under cover of the noise they produce, Betha leaves the hall unperceived, and seeks refuge in the ante-chamber.

'Just listen to those Matthews !' exclaims lively Miss Ellery ; 'hammering away as if they were in a blacksmith's forge, Ada three bars behind Ella as usual—which do you bet gets in first, Betha ?' and then observing her companion's expression, she continues : 'What ! still in the dumps about your mother—what a baby you are ! The idea of bothering yourself about anything when

you've gained the five first prizes at the
Princess College.   Why it will be in the
papers, Betha—fancy that ! in the papers !
Mercy on us ! the whole of my family,
grandfathers and grandmothers included,
might go to Jericho if I could only win the
half of them.   German, French, Elocution,
Composition, and History ! You're disgust-
ingly clever, you know, Betha.   It's a
shame you should walk off with all the best
prizes in that way ; it's enough to make a
girl kick you !' concludes Miss Lively, with
a playful lunge in the direction of her schoolfellow.   But Betha does not smile in return.

'Never mind Harriet's nonsense,' says
Martha Kemyss, as she bends over her and
kisses her forehead ; ' I am sure you will find
your dear mother safe and well when you
get home.   She has, most likely, been detained by business.'

Mattie is a lovely girl of eighteen, the
picture of an Eastern houri—sweet-tempered

and lovable, but not over-burdened with brains. But Betha looks up to her gratefully.

'You are always so sweet and so kind, Mattie. You ought to have a happy life, for your great anxiety is to make others so ! It is this bitterly cold weather that makes me afraid for my dear mother ; you cannot think '—with a shudder—'how terribly she suffers when she gets an attack of the heart ! I would give anything to know that she is well. But Miss Denny says I cannot go home until the prizes have been given away.'

'Of course not, dear ! And think how disappointed Mrs. Durant would be to see you come back without them, Betha.'

The girl smiles faintly—she is but a girl after all—and she knows how proud her mother is of her attainments.

'Come on !' cries Miss Ellery, who has been peeping through a crack of the door. 'The Matthews have finished—thank goodness that's over !—and I can see old Cockatoo marshalling Denny up to the table with the prizes. I hope he will give me one. If he doesn't, I've got a splendid bread-pellet to shoot at his bald head. Feel it, Betha, it's as hard as a stone ! I've been kneading it for him all day !'

But in another minute the young lady's liveliness is subdued, as an under-teacher appears to conduct them in state to the presence of the bishop, who has been installed with becoming ceremony behind a table, piled up with volumes bound in red and blue. Who has not officiated or assisted at that dullest of all dull exhibitions—a school examination ? His Lordship of the Cockatoo Islands delivers a rambling, twaddling little speech with each volume, that makes Miss Denny coo, and the majority of the girls giggle, and works up poor Betha Durant's over-strung nerves to such a tension, that before she is called up for the fifth time, she has made a hundred resolves not to wait for the end of it. But it is over at last, and instead of mixing with the visitors, as she is expected to do, and exhibiting her prizes for the benefit of the college, Betha rushes into the ante-chamber, and throwing her books upon the table, commences hurriedly to reassume her walking attire.

'Betha dear! you must wait for a cab. You cannot carry all those books through the streets,' says Mattie Kemyss.

'I can't wait! I shall be half-way home before they send for it. I must go and see after mother!'

'But does not Miss Denny expect us all to take tea with her to-night?'

'I can't help what she expects! Mattie dear, don't try to detain me! I have been going mad with anxiety for the last two hours.'

She twists her scarf about her throat as she speaks, and turns towards the door.

'But your books!' cries Mattie.

' They must remain here till to-morrow, I cannot stay !' are Betha's vanishing words, as she hurries through the corridor and out into the chill evening air.

CHAPTER II.

'I WILL GO AFTER HER!'

It is about six o'clock, but the streets are as dark as at night. Crowds of pedestrians, stamping their feet, or holding their muffs to their faces, throng the pavement, eager to complete their Christmas purchases and return to their firesides as soon as possible.

It is 'seasonable weather,' they say consolingly, as they salute each other in passing, but they are glad to get out of it all the same. The boys have made slides along the pavement, and the roadways are a sheet of ice, so that traffic has become dangerous, alike for man and beast; and more than one poor cab-horse, struggling on its side, has attracted a little crowd of spectators, whose curiosity outweighs their sense of cold.

But Betha heeds nothing and nobody—not even her own uncertain footing. She is like a dog on the right track returning to his home, and looking neither to one side nor the other for fear of losing the scent. She winds her way amongst the crowd, almost running over the slippery pavement in her anxiety to make haste, and arrives at the portals of her father's house, panting and out of breath. Even then she is afraid of knocking at the door, lest the sound should startle her nervous and easily alarmed mother, but is obliged to content herself by ringing the bell, and dancing in an agony of impatience on the step until her summons is attended to. Simultaneously with the appearance of the servant, the question bursts from her lips : '**How** is mamma ?'

'Your mamma, miss,' is the answer ; '*she's gone !*'

'*Gone!*' echoes Betha in a tone of horror;
'gone *where?*'

'Oh, Miss Betha dear! this has been a
terrible day,' says a muffled voice from the
staircase; and Betha looks up and sees her
old nurse Bentham on the landing with her
apron to her eyes, and her little sister
Hyacinth hanging on the banisters, her
childish face brimming over with important
news.   The girl pushes her way into the
passage, and supports herself against the
wall.

'What is the matter?' she utters faintly;
'tell me the truth.   Is she *dead?*'

'*Dead!* lor no, my dear.   Don't go to
fancy such a thing! It ain't come to that
yet, please God.   But whatever will become
of the mistress on such a night as this I can't
think.   It's just enough to kill her, and no
mistake.'

'Where has she gone? Why did she go
out?   Why did you let her go?' demands the
girl, roused from her first dread fear.

Hyacinth, a beautiful sharp-looking imp of ten, with dark eyes and chestnut curls down to her waist, lays one finger on her lip, and with a look of ineffable wisdom, points with the other to the closed dining-room door. It is to warn her elder sister that the master of the house is likely to overhear their conversation.

'There's been an awful row,' she whispers in the parlance of chits in this slangy generation. 'Oh, Betha, if you had only been here! Come upstairs and we will tell you all about it.'

Betha needs no second invitation. Curiosity combined with a terrible fear that the end of all things has arrived, make her eager to hear what has occurred during her absence.

The 'awful row' is unfortunately no novelty to her or any of the household. The novel thing is to reach bedtime without having overheard one of Major and Mrs. Durant's wordy disputes; but her mother has never gone the length of leaving her home before.

'Oh, nurse! what is it all about?' she exclaims, weeping, as she finds herself alone with Bentham and her little sister.

'Well, my dearie! don't cry now, but it's just this! Your ma, she was going to dress and drive down to the college, and I had my orders to get Miss Hyacinth ready to go with her, when your pa, he came home, and——'

'Yes!' interrupts Hyacinth without ceremony, 'papa came home, Betha, and he went into mamma's dressing-room, and began to make an awful noise and stamp about, and we could hear him talking, couldn't we, Benty? and then papa banged the door and went down into the dining-room, and mamma followed him; and she cried and they had another row, oh! much worse than the first one; and then mamma came upstairs again and put on her bonnet and shawl and went out, and she says she'll never come back

again—never—never—never! not as long as
ever she lives she won't, will she, Benty?'

'Oh! Cinthy, it can't be true! you don't
know what you are talking about,' gasps
Betha.

The girl's filial love amounts to a passion ;
from her infancy her mother has been the
recipient of her truest and tenderest affection,
and from the moment she was able to com-
prehend the misery of her domestic life, she
has elevated her to the position of an idol.

' Indeed, Miss Betha, I'm afraid she's not
so mistook as you seem to imagine,' remarks
the old nurse, who has had the charge of
both these children from their cradles ; ' for
your poor ma, she seemed terrible put out, to
be sure. *I*'ve never seen her so bad before,
long as I've served her ; and the last words
she say to me was, " You'll never see me in
this house again, Bentham," says she, " not if
you live for another fifty years," says she.'

' But surely you asked her where she was
going, nurse !'

'Lor ! Miss Betha, it wouldn't have been
no manner of use. She didn't know herself,
poor lady.   She was all off her head-like,
with your pa's treatment of her, and ran out
into the snow, for all the world like a wild
thing.'

'Mother ! mother !' cries Betha, in a tone
of anguish. 'Oh ! where can she be on this
bitterly cold night ? It will kill her, nurse !
You know how strictly Dr. Field has forbidden her venturing out on foot in the
ice and snow. She will get an attack of
those terrible spasms—she will fall down and
die in the streets from exposure to such
weather.'

'Aye,' acquiesces the nurse, with the usual
style of consolation adopted by her class ; 'I
shouldn't wonder if she did, poor lady—that
is if she's heedless enough to keep on her
feet on such an evening. But let's hope, my
dear, as she'll have more consideration for
herself.'

The daughter's face becomes white and

strained as her nervous system is thus cruelly played upon, and she clutches the old woman's arm with an energy that considerably startles her.

'Why didn't you go with her, nurse? It was your duty to have done so! you know how ill and feeble darling mother is.'

'Lor! Miss Betha, I was only too willing to go along with her, but the master he wouldn't let me.'

'Yes! Betha,' interpolates the imp, 'Benty cried and asked mamma to let her go too; but papa stood across the passage like a bear, and declared that anybody who went with mamma or fetched her a cab or did anything for her, should be dismissed from his service without warning: and mamma told Benty that the kindest thing she could do for her was to stay here and look after *me;* didn't she, Benty?'

'Then *I* will go after her,' exclaims Betha, with decision.

CHAPTER III.

THE old nurse lifts her hands in amazement.

'*You*, Miss Betha! Lor, my dear! if your pa wouldn't let *me* go, do you suppose he'll give his consent to a child like you running about the streets alone at this time of night?'

'I shall not ask for his consent,' says the girl proudly. 'I shall act on my own authority.'

'Oh, Betha! don't be so stupid,' interposes Hyacinth, as she shakes back the curls from her selfish little face. 'You'll only get chilblains, and what good can you do mamma? She's just as well able to walk as you are.'

'Do you suppose I can lie down in my bed and sleep,' replies the elder girl, with scorn, 'unless I know that dear mother is well and safely sheltered? But it is only your ignorance, Cinthy, that makes you talk in such a heartless manner. You cannot understand the terrible risk that mother runs on such a night as this. No one shall prevent me from going to seek her!'

'I understand just as well as you,' says Hyacinth pertly, 'but mamma went out of her own accord. She wanted to go—she said so—didn't she, Benty?'

'Where will you go to find her, Miss Betha?' asks the servant, without heeding the younger child's query.

'I don't know. To every house she has ever entered until I hear some news of her.'

'She's sure to go and tell Mrs. Wallerton,' pipes Hyacinth.

'To be sure, Miss Betha. Miss Cinthy always has the right thing to say, bless her! There's no lady been more to this house during the last twelvemonth than Mrs. Wallerton. I'd certainly go there first to hear news of your poor ma. But you'll be sure to be back in good time—won't you, my dear ?'

'I don't know. I'm not sure. Don't worry me with useless questions,' cries Betha, impatiently, as she prepares to leave the nursery. 'All I can say is that I am going to look for mother, and I'll never come back again until I've found her.'

'But, Betha, do stop and tell me about the prizes first !' exclaims Hyacinth, hanging on to her sister's dress.

The only answer vouchsafed her curiosity is the violent jerk by which Betha disengages herself as she runs down the staircase. But when she reaches the hall a barrier presents itself to her design. The door of the dining-room is suddenly opened and Major Durant stands in her path.

It is evident at once from whom Hyacinth inherits her dark beauty. Major Durant possesses the same brilliant eyes and curling chestnut hair as his younger daughter. There is no trace of similitude between himself and Betha, and from the manner in which he scowls at her, the disparity would appear to be as much in their dispositions as their persons.

'Where are you going?' he demands sternly.

'I am going to mamma.'

'I forbid your doing so! Go back to the nursery.'

'Papa, someone *must* go and look after her. You know how long she has been ill, and how seriously the cold of such a night may affect her heart. It was cruel and wicked to let her go out in it. I must and I will follow her!'

'It was your mother's own wish to go, and she is quite old enough to look after herself. She left my house against my express orders to the contrary, and I forbid any member of my family holding communication with her until she returns to it.'

'She left the house because you have made her life so miserable that she cannot remain in it!' cries the girl, with flashing eyes.

'Do you mean to insult me, miss? How dare you speak to me in such a way?'

'I dare to speak the truth, papa! Do you think I am blind or deaf, that I do not understand that my poor mother is an un-happy woman? Why, there is not a servant in the house who does not know it, and pity her for it. And she has borne it for years—dear mother!—with the patience and good-ness of an angel, and now that she can bear it no longer, and you have driven her nearly mad, you want us all to turn against her, as you do. But I won't—I *won't*. I love my mother dearly—devotedly, and I will never forsake her—not even if she were in the wrong, which I know she isn't.'

Major Durant looks very uneasy. He shuffles his feet and changes colour, and lets his eyes rest anywhere but on his outspoken

daughter's face. It is not pleasant to be told
of our faults, boldly and undisguisedly, and
more especially when the rebuke comes from
the lips of a mentor so many years younger
than ourselves. And Major Durant hates
Betha at that moment in proportion to her
honesty.

'You have a very sharp tongue, young
lady, and you have inherited the gift of
making use of it,' he replies angrily ; 'but I
repeat my prohibition : I will have no open
scandal made of this business, and I refuse
to let you quit the house.'

'Then I must send a note to Dr. Field,'
says Betha decidedly. 'He has given me
strict orders to tell him if mother is ever
careless of his directions, and I know he will
say that it's enough to kill her to be wandering about the streets when they are covered
with ice and snow.'

Major Durant begins to feel very uncomfortable. Like all bullies, he is a coward,
and Dr. Field has already seen too much of

the inner working of his married life to make
the idea of his being appealed to on the
subject a pleasant one.   On how many occasions has the doctor not been summoned to
revive Mrs. Durant from those fits of ex-
haustion which usually follow the excitement
of their disagreements?   Once, did he not
warn the husband that if he could not better
control his temper and his language his wife's
death might lie at his door?   Yes; the
major *has* reason for not desiring the inter-
ference of the blunt and plain-spoken Dr.
Field.   He attempts, therefore, to treat the
whole matter in a lighter spirit.

'My dear child, I do wish you would
learn not to exaggerate one's little domestic
difficulties in this way.   It is a very bad
habit to get into. *Wandering about the streets!*
Rubbish! what will you imagine next?   Is
it likely your mamma would be such a fool!
She is more probably toasting herself by the
fireside of some acquaintance, whilst she
pours the whole story of my iniquities into

her sympathising ear. She'll be back again
before midnight, you may take your oath of
it. Come now! show yourself to be the
sensible girl you are. Go upstairs again and
dress for dinner, and come and take your
mother's place at the head of the table.'

' I cannot !' says Betha, determinately. ' I
must follow my mother.'

' Then I shall prevent your doing so.'

' Papa, you cannot prevent me. I am not
a child, remember ! I was sixteen on my
last birthday, and where mother's health and
safety are concerned, I refuse to be controlled
by you or anyone !'

' Oh, indeed ! Perhaps you are also aware
that, being a woman, and beyond the control
of your natural guardians, I am not compelled
to receive you back into my house if you
quit it without leave.'

' I know nothing about it, but I don't want
to come back unless mother comes too. My
lot for life is cast in with hers.'

' Go to your mother, then !' exclaims the

major loudly and passionately, as he throws
open the hall-door; 'but, remember, if you
once cross that threshold you never re-enter
my house. I give you your choice, Betha,
between your mother and myself. Follow
your own headstrong will if it pleases you,
but if you do so, against my express command to the contrary, I will never receive
you as my daughter again!'

'I must follow my mother!' cries the girl,
as she runs lightly past her father down the
flight of stone steps into the little garden,
and so out into the gathering blackness of
the winter's night.

CHAPTER IV.

'TAKE THAT WOMAN AWAY.'

FOR a few minutes Betha runs on, heedless of what direction her feet shall take, until she finds herself in the glare of the lighted shops, and under the scrutiny of a crowd of strangers; then she stops suddenly, and assuming a soberer pace, tries to collect her scattered thoughts and consider what is best to be done. There is no fear nor indecision in the girl's mind : no regret for the harsh words with which she has been driven from her father's door; she has but one idea in her brain—where best to turn in order to find her mother ! Her youthful appearance and ignorance of the world are the only childish

things about Betha Durant. In reasoning
faculty and mental strength she is in advance
of many women of twice her age; and the
unhappy occurrence that has taken place in
her own home to-day, seems to have forced
into fruition every power she possesses.

As she halts, ostensibly to look into a shop
window, in reality to press her hand against
her brow and decide upon her course of
action, she feels far more like a mother
going in search of her child, than a child
bent upon finding its mother. The words
of the nurse and Hyacinth concerning Mrs.
Wallerton recur to her mind. There is no
doubt of their accuracy. Mrs. Wallerton is
the most intimate friend her mother possesses. During the past year she has been
constantly at the house, running in and out,
without invitation, at all sorts of odd moments,
and bringing the most charming presents of
flowers and fruit to tempt the appetite of the
invalid.

Betha has often seen Mrs. Wallerton hang

over Mrs. Durant, and kiss her, and call her
her ‘ dearest Mary !’ has even heard the
lively widow take the major roundly to
task for neglecting his wife, or refusing to
believe in her illness, until her mother's
cheeks have been crimson with shame and
mortification. There is no doubt in Betha's
mind, but that Mrs. Wallerton likes her
mother as much as she professes to do, and
that she is the person to whom Mrs. Durant
would be most likely to fly for protection and
advice in a moment of distress. Betha has
scarcely settled this point satisfactorily in her
own mind, before she finds herself in front
of Mrs. Wallerton's house, which is situated
at no great distance from Northallerton
Crescent.

As she enters the hall and asks hurriedly
for the mistress, she can see, through the
open door of the dining-room, the table laid
for dinner, gay with hothouse flowers and
bright with silver and cut glass, for Mrs.
Wallerton is rich and luxurious in her tastes,

and loves to spend her money on herself.
She runs down the stairs as she hears
Betha's voice in the hall, and draws her
visitor into the privacy of the dining-
room.

'My dearest girl! What brings you here
on such a terrible evening?'

Mrs. Wallerton, standing under the full
blaze of the gaslight, presents the picture of
a handsome woman of about thirty. She is
tall, full-bosomed and broad-shouldered, with
a waist of five-and-twenty inches—that owes
its size to compression rather than to Nature,
a fact that is evidenced by the stiffness of
her figure and the flush upon her face, though
the widow stoutly denies it. Her Irish na-
tionality is betrayed in her dark, coarse hair,
and her prominent eyes and heavy jaw. But
she has small white even teeth and ripe pout-
ing lips, and a certain fascination of manner
that is very attractive to such people as have
not the power to look below the surface.
This fascination is greatly enhanced by the

fact that Mrs. Wallerton's conscience is of
that easy description that permits her to lie
without scruple, whilst she has her wits suffi-
ciently about her to prevent her lies being
found out. To utter a falsehood is as natural
to those cherry lips as to say 'good-morning ;'
indeed, so long and faithfully has she practised
the art, that it has become a second nature
to her.

How many ladylike liars do we not meet
as we pass through the world! They are the
poison of society—that make it the vile sham
it is of subterfuge, and backbiting, and un-
truth—yet they possess the ablest weapon
with which to cut their own way through it :
the power of appearing all things to all men.
Each one of Mrs. Wallerton's acquaintances,
whilst listening eagerly to her carefully
veiled detraction of the rest, believes firmly
that she is true at least to her listener. And
each one is gulled in turn. So how should
Betha, fresh from her schoolroom experience,
think otherwise than that all the honeyed

words proceeding from that sweetly smiling mouth are true.

'Oh! Mrs. Wallerton,' she exclaims, hurriedly, 'is mother with you?'

'Your mother, Betha! No! Why—what makes you ask me such an extraordinary question?'

The girl has made up her mind so firmly that she will be successful in her search, that the disappointment overcomes her.

'She has left home,' she replies, sobbing. 'Papa has been unkind to her again, dreadfully, cruelly unkind; and she has run away, and no one knows where she has gone to.'

At the receipt of this intelligence the widow's face grows dark, and she bites her lip sharply to hide her evident annoyance.

'Run away! Betha! Impossible! Some one has exaggerated the truth to you! Were you at home when it occurred? What did your papa say to make her so angry?'

'I don't think she was angry, Mrs. Wallerton, only very unhappy about something. It is nurse who told me the story. I was at college at the time; it is our examination-day, you know, and I knew nothing of it until I returned home. But indeed it is true, for papa told me so himself, and he ordered me not to follow her; but I was too frightened to obey him.'

'And you imagined you would find your mamma with me, my dear ?'

'I could not tell. You have always been so kind to mother, Mrs. Wallerton; I thought she would think of you first. And now I don't know where to go, or what to do.'

The widow's face is portentously grave. It is pleasant for an independent woman to have admirers floating in an easy, nonchalant manner about her, but not so agreeable to be suddenly wakened to the truth that her careless flirtations are likely to be made the occasion of a public scandal.

'I wish Mrs. Durant *had* come here,' she says. 'Betha, you have distressed me beyond measure with this news. I have such a high respect for your dear mamma, and indeed for your papa also, that these domestic quarrels shock me terribly. I have not been used to them; they are matters altogether beyond my sphere of cognisance. Why cannot people live happily and pleasantly together, as they were intended to do? Not that I have the least wish to blame either your mamma or your papa, my dear. They must know their own affairs best. Only it is so terrible for their friends. But it cannot last. They have fallen out over some little trifle, may be; but depend upon it, that in a day or two they will come to see their folly, and all will be right again between them.'

'I don't know : I can't say, Mrs. Wallerton. But meanwhile, where can mother be? Oh! I am so frightened for her in all this frost and snow.'

'No doubt she has gone to your aunt, Mrs. Chapman. I wonder it did not strike you before, Betha. Mrs. Durant is far more likely to go to Earl's Court than to come to me.'

'To Aunt Janie! But she lives so many miles away.

'My dear child, a cab will take you there in half-an-hour. But stay ; sit down for two minutes, and I will take you there myself.'

'But you have not had your dinner yet!'

'Never mind my dinner. It must wait for a little while.'

'Oh, Mrs. Wallerton! how kind you are!'

'Not at all, my dear! Do you think I would allow you to go alone? Your papa ought to be taking you himself, but as he is such a naughty man, I will try and fill his place. And I would do anything in the world for your dear mother, Betha,' continued the widow, in a lower voice, ' and shall not be satisfied till I know where she is. Have a glass of wine before we go ! It will do you good !'

As Mrs. Wallerton utters these words, and encircles the drooping girl's form with her arms, Betha thinks she is the kindest and most sympathetic friend they have ever possessed; and as they drive together, as fast as the state of the roads will permit them, towards the house of Mrs. Chapman, Mrs. Wallerton blames her father's conduct openly to her young companion, and declares she shall not rest day nor night until she sees his domestic relationship restored to its former basis.

'Such a dear, sweet creature as your mamma is, too, Betha! I am sure I could not venture to say what I have to the child of any other woman, but then you are so sensible and beyond your years. You take so much after her in every respect, you will be able to understand the feeling that dictates my words. But to see a person like her unappreciated, so elegant, so refined, and so amiable, cuts me to the very soul, Betha, and I can't think what your papa can be made of, to be so shortsighted. I shall not rest until we have found her—be sure of that! and if she is not at your aunt's, we will drive round London all night long, until we have discovered her hiding-place.

Betha presses the soft, plump hand that holds her own, and feels as if she had indeed found a friend in need.

As their cab draws up before the door of Mrs. Chapman's house, a sober-coloured brougham, which they do not perceive in the darkness, moves slowly onward to make way for them ; and before they have time to knock, a maid-servant, evidently on the watch, quietly opens the hall-door, and admits them.

' Is Mrs. Durant here ?' asks Betha, breathlessly.

' Yes, miss ! she is, but——'

Betha waits for no explanation. In the same moment she has pushed open a door on the ground-floor and stands upon the threshold of the room. The first glance tells her the whole story. On the sofa, with closed eyes, is extended the form of Mrs. Durant, whilst by her side sits Dr. Field, and over her bends Mrs. Chapman. Pillows, a blanket, mustard, brandy, and a faint pervading odour of eau-de-Cologne, give the usually neat apartment the semblance of a sick-room, and Betha's worst fears are realised. For well she recognises the accompaniments of the complaint : her mother has been suffering from an attack of the heart.

' Mother—darling mother !' she exclaims impulsively ; ' Mrs. Wallerton has brought me to you !'

A prolonged ' *Hush !*' comes simultaneously from the lips of both doctor and nurse as they turn and perceive the new presence in the room—but it comes too late. Mrs. Durant has heard her daughter's words, and before they can prevent her, she has risen to a sitting posture. Her eyes gleam like living fire, and her cheeks glow with the sudden excitement.

' Take her away !' she screams, as she points with one white thin hand in the direction of the buxom widow ; ' I will not speak to her ! It is she that has done it all ! It is she that has killed me !'

' Dearest Mary, pray compose yourself ! pray lie down !' says Mrs. Chapman, per-

suasively, but the sick lady continues to cry,
' Take that woman away—take her away !'

' Betha stands horror-struck between the
two. What has occurred ? Has her poor
mother lost her senses, that she should speak
to her best friend in so extraordinary a
manner ? Before she has time to speculate
on the probable answer to her question, her
aunt Janie advances to Mrs. Wallerton.

' I must ask you to retire,' she says, in a
voice which seems to Betha unnecessarily
harsh. ' My sister is very ill indeed, and quite
unfit to see strangers.'

' *Strangers !*' echoes the widow, ' I should
think I could hardly be classed in such a
category, considering that I have left my
dinner-table on a night like this to bring Mrs.
Durant's daughter to her side. It is the
first time I have ever heard myself spoken of
as a " stranger " before, either by the lady or
any of her family, and I must say her conduct is rather inexplicable to me.'

For still the cry of ' Take her away !' is

sounding from Mrs. Durant's pale lips, whilst
Dr. Field is doing all he can to calm and
pacify her.

'I have no doubt it is,' replies Mrs. Chapman, who has contrived to edge her visitor
outside the door; 'but she is dangerously ill,
as you may see, she hardly knows what she
is saying; and at all hazards we must try and
keep her from further excitement. Indeed
it will be kinder of you to leave us alone!'

'Oh! I have no desire to intrude—it is
not my nature,' replies the widow, shrugging
her shoulders; 'of course, I have done a
great deal for poor Mrs. Durant from time to
time, and I was actuated by the purest pity
in coming here to see her to-night; still, if
my presence is not welcome, I can but be
sorry and withdraw it. I hope to have better
accounts of her in the morning. Good-night,
Betha dear!'

But Betha cannot with sincerity return the
salutation. Those terrible mysterious words,
'*It is she that has killed me,*' are still sound-

ing in her ears, and she is leaning, sick and
faint with astonishment and wonder, against
her mother's couch.

'Mother, mother dearest! don't you know
me?' she wails in a low voice. The agony
which succeeded her recognition of Mrs.
Wallerton has passed again, and Mrs. Durant
is lying back on the pillows, looking as white
and exhausted as a lily beaten down by the
rain.'

'Yes, child! yes!' she replies faintly, 'you
are Betha! But never let me see you with
that woman again.'

'My dear lady, I cannot allow you to
excite yourself,' says the doctor, in a voice of
warning.

'Very well, doctor, I will not speak of it;
but you must let me talk to Betha. Betha
dear, it is all over; the end is coming fast
now!'

'Oh, mother, mother! don't say that!'

Was this, then, to be the reward of her
loving search? To find her mother pale and

exhausted, her face covered with the sweat
of death ; the fierce agony over, but her poor
worn-out heart beating fainter and fainter
with each laboured respiration.   The girl has
often seen her, apparently as prostrated as
she is now ; but something tells her—perhaps
the unmistakable look in the eyes of the
dying, perhaps the mercy of a watchful,
though invisible guardian—that this will be
the last time, and she feels stricken dumb
with the agony of despair.

'But it is true ! This has finished it all.
His conduct, the ice, the snow. I have
suffered such unutterable anguish ; but I am
quiet now.   May he treat my poor children
better than he has treated me ! Oh, my
Hyacinth ! my darling, my best-loved child !
What pain it is to leave her !'

The true, brave heart of the daughter,
leaning over the dying woman's couch, seems
suddenly to stop. Yes ; this has been the
unrecognised, though not unfelt, disappointment of her girlish life. She has loved her

mother with entire devotion—as the one great object of her existence, and her mother's best affections have been lavished on her younger child. Betha has been the ever-ready sympathiser and nurse and friend, but pert, pretty Hyacinth, with her sharp tongue and her gipsy curls, has been the pride and darling of Mrs. Durant's life. And now the last few precious moments of that life are to be devoted to her.

'Betha, take care of Cinthy!' she gasps. 'Be a mother to her! My sweet child! Try and supply my place! Don't let her miss me. And yet she *must* miss her loving mother's care—my beautiful darling! Oh, my God! it is so hard not to see her again!'

'Shall I go and fetch her?' exclaims Betha, anxious only to please her mother; but a warning look from Dr. Field silences her again.

'Too—late!' murmurs Mrs. Durant faintly, and then she puts out her hand and feebly draws Betha's face to hers, and so lies

4—2

silent, whilst the others stand beside, watching each breath, as it is drawn more and more lingeringly from her ashen-grey lips.

'Cinthy!—be good to Cinthy!' she whispers presently, and Betha, kissing her passionately, assures her that she will.

And then Mrs. Durant turns her head two or three times on the pillow, as though to settle herself into an easier position, gives a soft, contented sigh, and with a faint smile on her lips, gently droops her lids upon her eyes.

'She is asleep,' whispers Betha, turning her tear-stained face towards the doctor.

He has his finger on the patient's pulse, and for a moment he does not answer her. Only he raises his eyes to meet those of Mrs. Chapman, and, with a grave look, replaces the hand he holds upon the breast of Mrs. Durant.

'You had better come away, darling,' says Mrs. Chapman, as she attempts to raise Betha from the floor.

' Oh no! Aunt Janie, let me sit and watch by her till she wakes. I will be as quiet as a mouse, and the time is so short, you know '—with a gasping sob—' she might want me. I cannot bear to leave her for a minute.'

' My darling Betha, she will never want you again. It's all over !' says Mrs. Chapman, bursting into tears.

' *What !*' cries the girl, springing to her feet.

' Your dear mother is gone, my child,' interposes Dr. Field; for Aunt Janie is sobbing too much to speak. ' She is dead! Try not to grieve too much, Betha ! She has suffered from heart-disease for many years past, and in any case the end could not have been much longer delayed.'

' *Gone !*—gone, *already !*' cries Betha, in a tone of the keenest anguish. ' And she never said she loved me !'

The shock, the excitement, and the fatigue
of the day have been too much for her, and
as the last words leave her lips, she sinks
unconscious on the floor.

CHAPTER V.

'I HAVE DECIDED.'

FOR a few days after her mother's death, Betha's senses are mercifully dulled to all earthly things. She is not unconscious; she is perfectly aware that her idol is dead, and that she shall never speak to her again; that *that* which lies so silent and immovable in the next room is deaf and insensible to all that she may say or do. She knows it, but she cannot realise it. She cannot identify that marble image with the mother she has lost. Her aunt Janie wants her to go and look at it and cry over it, and kiss it, hoping thereby that the girl's emotion may be excited, and a more natural state of things set in. But Betha is as yet incapable of the comfort of tears. She lies on her bed, with dry eyes and listless limbs, thinking neither of the past nor the future—forgetting even to blame her father for his conduct—only desirous to be left alone, and not worried to eat, or drink, or talk, that she may try to make her brain obey her will, and understand that she is parted from her dearest friend, in this world, for ever.

Mrs. Chapman, on the other hand, is all energy and excitement. There is so much to be done and to be said, with such a dreadful occurrence as her ' own dear sister actually dying in her very dining-room,' so much re-crimination to be levelled at the head of her offending brother-in-law, and so much discussion about the funeral and dear Betha's prospects, and the shocking suspicions she entertains concerning that horrid woman, Mrs. Wallerton, that she is regaling her visitors with the history all day long.

'Yes, indeed, Mrs. Jones !' she will say, as

she hangs tearfully over the body of her departed sister, 'poor dear Mary *had* a life of it, and no mistake. If you had only seen her suffer, as I have! How she could stand it so long is a marvel to me! Often and often I've said to her, "Why not leave the man? Why stay in the house to be ill-treated and insulted as you are?" But she was so patient, so uncomplaining—never a word to anyone; but of course she could not hide it from me. I am sure she had the goodness of an angel.'

'But is it true that the poor dear died in the snow?' says Mrs. Jones. 'My maid tells me the report is all over Kensington.'

'Oh no; it was not quite so bad as that; but she arrived here in so exhausted a condition, we had not even time to move her upstairs. There is no doubt the exposure to the cold hastened her end; it brought on one of those fearful attacks of spasms that are so fatal in heart-disease; and then, darling Mary was so imprudent. She walked here,

all the way from Regent's Park, and with
thin house-boots on.   I don't think she knew
what she was doing, poor dear!   Her mind
was quite upset by Major Durant's brutal
conduct to her.   We sent for the doctor at
once, but he could do nothing for her.   Her
screams were heartrending.   And then Betha
arrived with that horrid Mrs. Wallerton, and
it excited Mary so that she never rallied
afterwards.   Oh, it has been a terrible affair,
Mrs. Jones!—a most terrible and heartrending affair!—and I don't feel as if I should
ever get over it!' concludes Mrs. Chapman,
sobbing.

She is very like her dead sister, both in
appearance and disposition, and both women
are   weak,   washed-out   representatives   of
Betha.   It is from her mother that the girl
has inherited her ripe-corn-coloured hair and
grey eyes—only Mrs. Durant's eyes were of
a pale grey, and her hair was faded and limp.
Her character, too, was more yielding and
amiable than that of her high-spirited daugh-

ter, with less courage and energy and less power of affection.

Aunt Janie is a prototype of **Mrs. Durant.** She is one of those enthusiastic, warm-hearted, fickle-minded people, who take up the cause of another as though it were their own so long as their partisanship does not affect their interests, and drop it like a hot coal as soon as it does. She advances to the fight like a hero, but as soon as she en-counters any opposition she retreats like a craven. She has always been ready to fondle her sister and moan over her troubles, but she has never tried to help her out of them, either by counsel or action. She can weep copiously over her now she is dead, but living, her friendship proved but a broken reed. So, she can weep copiously over Betha at the present moment, and make grand plans for her future ; but it remains to be proved what her action will be, when that future has turned into the present.

‘ That poor girl upstairs,’ sighs Mrs. Jones,

'she is old enough to feel all this terribly!
How will she meet her father?'

'She shall *never* meet him!' exclaims Mrs.
Chapman, energetically. 'She has received
too much ill-treatment at his hands already.
Why, Mrs. Jones, the man actually told her
that if she went in search of her poor dying
mother he would never receive her as a
daughter again.   It curdles my blood to
think of it, and I don't feel as if I could even
speak to Major Durant.   He must come
here for the funeral, I suppose, but it is the
last time he enters my house, and I shall tell
him so without reserve.'

'You will do very right!' exclaims Mrs.
Jones.

'And as for Betha, she will be *my* child
henceforward — as much mine as Blanche.
The only difference will be that I shall have
two daughters to love me instead of one.'

And Aunt Janie, who is a widow, calls
her only child to her side, and with tears in
her eyes conjures her to take her motherless

cousin to her heart as a sister, and never look upon her thenceforward in any other light.

'My own sweet Mary's legacy to me,' she exclaims, as she folds both the girls in her maternal arms. 'Betha, you must try and look on me as a mother now, for I will never let you return to that wicked man's roof again—never, so long as you live!'

'Thank you, dear Aunt Janie. I—I— should like to remain with you for a little while, if I may. I don't think I *could* go back again just yet—not—not—while everything is so difficult to forget.'

'You shall *never* go back,' repeats Aunt Janie, determinately. 'You must meet him I suppose, on the day of the funeral; but when that is over you shall return home with me, and be Blanche's sister as long as you live.'

'Hyacinth,' falters Betha, in a tone of remonstrance; but she is too weary and too sick at heart to argue the point, and Aunt

Janie is satisfied that she shall have her own way.

The day of the funeral arrives. The coffin, with its silent inmate, has been carried downstairs, preparatory to being lifted into the hearse, and Mrs. Chapman, who, with Betha, has arranged to attend the ceremony, is advised that Major Durant and Dr. Field are waiting her presence in the diningroom.

'Come, darling!' she says, as she throws the deep crape veil over Betha's mourning bonnet, and draws the girl's hand through her arm; 'take courage! It will soon be over, and you shall not even speak to Major Durant if you do not wish to do so.'

But as they enter the room where the funeral guests are assembled Betha gives a cry of surprise and terror, and hides her face upon the bosom of her aunt.

Mrs. Chapman looks up, astounded, to encounter the form, decorously draped in the deepest mourning, of Mrs. Wallerton.

' Is this intended for an insult ?' she cries involuntarily.

The face of everyone in the room changes. If there is one thing in this world more unpleasant to be mixed up with than another it is a domestic difference, and especially on such a solemn occasion as a funeral.

'I don't understand you,' says Mrs. Wallerton, quickly. 'I have come here, on the invitation of Major Durant, to pay the last respect I can to his departed wife, who was one of my dearest friends. Have you any objections to make to it ?'

Aunt Janie is already defeated. Her spark of courage is extinguished. She does not know how to continue the contest.

'I don't think my poor sister considered you as her dearest friend,' she answers, in a more subdued voice.

'I am astonished you should open such a discussion at such a moment,' interposes Major Durant, offendedly. 'Whatever my late wife may have said or thought, the fact speaks for itself : Mrs. Wallerton's kindness to the whole of my family has been unvarying, and were it not a most improper moment for disputing the matter, I should certainly call on you, Mrs. Chapman, to make her an apology for the words you have just spoken.'

'Pray let us have no quarrelling,' says Dr. Field, 'and especially in this presence. I think we are all assembled. Had we not better set out for the cemetery at once ?'

'Come, dear Betha,' says her aunt, encouragingly.

'No, no !' exclaims the girl, shrinking back. 'I cannot go—I will not go !'

'Hush, my love !' whispers Mrs. Chapman ; 'gloss it over, as I have done. The least said, the soonest mended !'

'*I will not go !*' repeats the girl, resolutely.

'What is all this fuss about ?' demands Major Durant, with flashing eyes.

'I am afraid dear Betha is ill. She does not feel equal to attending the ceremony,' says Mrs. Chapman.

' I am not ill,' exclaims the girl, standing upright, and facing the assembly, ' but I cannot go with *Mrs. Wallerton!*'

' How dare you !' commences her father, angrily; but the doctor draws him on one side and entreats him to be silent and let the funeral proceed.

So the bearers are summoned, and the Silent Presence is marshalled out of the room before them, followed by a wailing cry of ' Mother ! mother !' which rings in the ears of more than one of the mourners during the succeeding solemnity. And the guests file after it and get into their carriages, and Betha is left alone in the dining-room with her face hidden in her hands.

After a long, long interval of two hours Aunt Janie returns, her eyelids swollen and her crape veil limp with her tears ; but now that she is relieved of the presence of the enemy, full of righteous indignation against Major Durant and Mrs. Wallerton, and determined that Betha shall never return to her father's protection again.

'It is impossible, my dear; he will subject you to the presence of that woman every day, and you know how your poor mamma disliked her. It is an insult to her memory. I don't feel as if she would lie quiet in her grave if you make friends with Mrs. Wallerton.'

'Oh no, no! Indeed I could not! I shall never forget the last words my darling mother said about her. But, Aunt Janie, I must go back some time—because of Hyacinth, you know.'

'You will do no such thing! You will remain with me and be my child. Promise me, Betha — promise that you will never leave me.'

'I don't wish to leave you, dear Aunt Janie. I should like to live here for ever, only——'

At this juncture Major Durant is announced, and enters the room. He looks dark and angry, and refuses to take the seat that Mrs. Chapman offers him.

'I dare say you are surprised to see me here again, Mrs. Chapman,' he commences stiffly; 'but I wish to have this matter settled at once. My daughter Elizabeth has behaved very badly to me—very badly indeed——'

'You behaved very badly to her,' rejoins Aunt Janie.

'We will let that pass, if you please. A child is no judge of the actions of its father. Elizabeth left my house against my orders, and with the knowledge that I should refuse to receive her again. But for late circumstances 1 should have adhered to that determination. But since Mrs. Durant's death leaves the girl without a natural protector, I am willing, upon certain conditions, to take her home with me.'

'Betha refuses to return to Northallerton Crescent under any conditions,' says Mrs. Chapman.

'Pardon me! but I must hear her determination from her own lips. She is no longer a child (as she has taken care to inform me), and must, therefore, be quite competent to give expression to her sentiments.'

'What are the conditions ?' demands Betha, as she raises her heavy eyes to confront her father.

As the man meets his daughter's gaze, a sudden chill seems to strike through his frame : she looks so like his wife as he saw her for the last time before the coffin-lid was closed ; and something, not quite dead yet, pricks his uneasy conscience.

'Not very hard ones, Betha !' he answers; 'simply, that you shall behave to me as a daughter should do, and receive my friends as your own. But I must have no airs and graces, mind you ! no allusions to the past, nor rubbish of that sort. You must act as a sensible girl, or I won't have you at all.'

'Must I be friendly with—with—*that woman ?*'

' Whom do you mean by " that woman " ?' cries the major, fiercely.

' Mrs. Wallerton !'

' Of course you must! why, what confounded rubbish is this ? The best and truest friend your mother had—who visited her oftener and gave her more presents than anyone else—and now you have got some absurd crotchet in your head against her. I won't have it, I say ! Mrs. Wallerton will always be an honoured and welcome guest in my house, and whoever lives there will have to receive her as such.'

' I cannot—I cannot !' sobs Betha, vehemently ; ' she killed my mother. They were her last words, that Mrs. Wallerton had killed her ; and I will not shake hands with her nor speak to her again !'

' Then stay where you are !' cries her father, angrily.

He has grown very pale at his daughter's open announcement, but he stands to his ground. Perhaps he expected to hear some-

thing of the sort—perhaps it is not the first
time he has heard it—anyway he bears the
shock bravely.

'That she certainly shall do,' interposes
Aunt Janie, who can be courageous where
she has to back an assertion instead of re-
futing it. 'Betha and I arrived at that conclusion some days ago, so you might have
spared yourself the trouble of questioning
her.'

'But she must understand the alternative,'
exclaims the major. 'If she refuses to return to me now, I shall never give her
another opportunity. She may starve in the
gutter, or beg her bread from door to door.
I will have nothing further to do with her
from this day.'

'Betha desires nothing better,' commences
Mrs. Chapman defiantly, but the girl interrupts her.

'Hyacinth!' she utters with trembling
lips ; 'may I not see her sometimes ?'

'Certainly not !' returns her father ; ' I

will not have the only child left to me contaminated by your evil example, and set against my best friends. There will be no communication of any sort permitted between you.'

'Oh! what shall I do? What *shall* I do?' exclaims Betha in a voice of despair.

As she sits there, with clasped hands and downcast eyes, trying to decide upon her path of action, a vision rises before her of her dead mother, lying still and saintly in her coffin, with an aureole of pale hair about her brow and the snow-wreaths on her grave —and then of the blooming widow with flushed cheeks and sparkling eyes, and a rustling of silk and a redolence of patchouli about her—and she shrinks as though she had stepped upon an adder!

'Stay with us, darling!' murmurs Aunt Janie in her ear. 'You cannot return home under present circumstances. Remember your poor mother, and stay with us.'

'Yes, yes! I have decided! Aunt Janie, I will remain with you!'

'Then all is over between us,' says Major Durant, as he quits the room.

'No mother and no father!' sobs Betha in Mrs. Chapman's arms; 'oh, Aunt Janie, it does seem hard—but I could not go back to that house again—after what *she* said.'

'Hush, Betha! never speak of that, my dear. It is best we should try and forget it. And don't say you have no mother! *I* am your mother, dearest, until my life ends.'

CHAPTER VI.

IT is useless for kind friends to come and remonstrate with Mrs. Chapman at that early period on the attitude she has assumed towards Major Durant, nor the responsibility she undertakes in persuading her niece not to return to Northallerton Crescent. Aunt Janie is too enthusiastic on the subject of her new toy to be able to see the force of any arguments brought to bear against her resolution. She laughs at the idea of Betha ever proving too expensive, or too troublesome, or too anxious a charge for her small means and smaller brains. Mrs. Chapman is the widow of an army surgeon, living with her only child on a very slender pittance, in a very tiny house in the Earl's Court district. She has often known what it is to be pinched for means, and compelled to give up the comforts of this lower existence; still her gushing affectionate heart, and her weak and quickly impressed brain, continue between them to make her believe that an extra mouth to feed and an extra body to clothe will not make their demands felt by her slender purse.

Perhaps Aunt Janie expects a miracle to be performed for the special benefit of herself and Betha, and indeed she can be very pious at times, and quote texts about the ravens and the widow's cruse of oil, that would make a stranger to her disposition really think that she had kept Betha at Earl's Court for the sake of befriending the girl, instead of for the pleasure of gratifying herself. Aunt Janie never gives one thought to the supposition that she may be seriously injuring the future prospects of her niece. She only recognises the fact that her present conduct is calling forth a host of arguments from her more sensible friends, and a host of small flatteries from the weak-minded ones.

'It is useless to discuss the point with me,' says Aunt Janie, with her sweetest smile, 'for I have reasons for my present action that cannot possibly be overthrown by any worldly consideration. I feel that I am only carrying out what would have been my dear dead sister's last wishes had she been able to express them, and that darling Mary would never rest quiet in her grave if I allowed Betha to return to the power of that inhuman monster, Major Durant!'

To this touching sentiment most of Mrs. Chapman's friends purr a sympathetic acquiescence, but a few say, 'Humph!' and amongst the few is Dr. Field. He has known Betha Durant for many years, and giving her credit for all her cleverness, with not one half her strength of mind, he believes that hers is one of the most dangerous tem-

peraments that can possibly be exposed to
the tempest of the world.

' Better a thousand times,' he thinks to
himself, ' that that girl should endure however unhappy a home with her father, than
be left to the fickle mercies of Mrs. Chapman, or be cast adrift to earn her own
living.'

With which idea he draws so vivid a
picture for Aunt Janie of the weight and
responsibility of the burthen she has taken
on herself, that it sinks deep into her mind.

She will not acknowledge the reason of it
at the time (when does a silly woman ever
acknowledge the reason of anything ?), but
it returns upon her, little by little, as the
days go on, and not always unaccompanied
by a twinge of fear lest the doctor should
after all prove to be right, and she to have
done both a foolish and a hasty action.

And Betha's conscience, too, is not altogether free of offence. She knows nothing
as yet, poor child, of butchers' and bakers'

bills, and almost as little of a young lady's
annual expenses for amusements and dress.
At sixteen all such anxieties are taken off
a girl's shoulders by her mother or her
guardian : and they are still amongst the
pleasures to come for Elizabeth Durant.
She has always been fed and clothed and
educated without any reference to herself,
and she does not suppose that she will be
any more trouble to her aunt than she has
been to her parents. No! it is of Hyacinth
that she thinks : of the little sister who was
so dear to her dead mother : and to whom
she commissioned her with her last breath
to be a friend, and an example, and a
guide.

Betha sheds many bitter tears when she
remembers the pert brat who has been the
trouble and the nuisance of her life hitherto,
but who now appears, by the force of those
dying words, to be transformed into something as near and as dear as a child of her
own.

She often cries for a sight of Cinthy half through the night, although she hardly believes that she will be parted from her long. Her father will relent—Mrs. Wallerton will go away—something will happen to make all things straight again—that is, as far as they can be straight whilst her darling mother is lying in the grave.

The girl fights hard with her grief. She is not the sort of girl to sit down idly and nurse it with futile tears and lamentations. She has her own pet theories about this world and the next, and believes fully that the separation is one of sight only and not of spirit. Yet it is very hard to bear. Each day seems to increase rather than diminish the pain of missing her mother, as though she had mourned first only her temporary absence, fully expecting her after a while to return, and was but waking up, hour by hour, to the fatal truth that their parting in this world is for ever.

Aunt Janie is very judicious at this period.

She allows Betha to spend her time pretty much as she chooses, and so the weeks flew by smoothly and quietly enough. Her cousin Blanche is the great drawback to her material comfort. This young lady, who is a couple of years older than Betha, and has been allowed by her weak-minded mother to have her own way in everything, cannot possibly understand how her cousin will ever recover herself if she sits moping in her own room all day, reading musty old books from the small library her papa left behind him. To Miss Blanche, a novelty in art needle-work, or a walk to Kensington High Street, or a visit to friends—since such are the only dissipations of which deep mourning will permit—would appear a much more sensible way of diverting one's mind.

But Betha does not care for needlework, and shrinks from the sight of strangers, and seems to take no interest in anything except those old volumes which neither the widow nor the daughter of Dr. Chapman have ever thought it worth their while to dislodge from the shelves on which he left them.

'And such dry things, too! Plays, of all horrors!' cries Miss Blanche one day in March, as she discovers Betha poring over an obsolete edition of Colley Cibber's plays. 'What can you find to interest you in them?'

'*Dry*, Blanche? Indeed they are not! Such fine old plays: full of bold language and strong situations!'

'Oh, bother your strong situations, Betha! Come down and have a strong cup of tea— that's much more likely to do you good! And Bobby Frere's in the drawing-room, telling us such tales about that old quiz, his grandmother! It'll kill you to listen to them.'

'Mr. Frere!' repeats Betha, shrinking a little backwards. 'Oh, I wish he wouldn't come here!'

'That's a polite speech, I must say, of one of mamma's guests,' replies Blanche, laughing. 'Why, the Freres are amongst our oldest friends. But you needn't mind *him*, I am sure, Betha! Nobody ever thinks anything of Bobby Frere.'

'I think your compliment is rather the worst one of the two, Blanche,' says Betha, with a faint smile, as she lays down her book and prepares to follow her cousin to the drawing-room. Mr. Robert Frere would certainly not present a formidable appearance to any young lady out of her teens, for he is one of the ugliest and most awkward specimens of the human race ever seen. He is tall and lanky, and high-shouldered, with very short-sighted, soft brown eyes; a large nose and mouth, and long, well-shaped feet and hands. His face has a clever and resolute appearance when in repose, but becomes almost ludicrous when he attempts to smile; and as he always smiles when he catches sight of Betha, he usually presents himself before her in the character of a 'wide-mouthed, gaping frog.' An astute observer

would tell you that Robert Frere's soft,
womanly eyes are sufficient to redeem the
rest of his features from the charge of ugliness, and that each lineament of his face
bears upon it the impress of a tender and
loving spirit.   But Betha has not yet learned
to be astute.   She only sees the outer man,
and like most very young girls, because the
outer man expresses pleasure at the sight of
her, she is half afraid of him, she scarcely
knows why.   She thinks him hideous, and
says so openly, although Aunt Janie has more
than once rebuked her for the assertion, re-
minding her that Robert Frere, being the
only son of Sir Willoughby Frere, of Baron's
Court, who is as wealthy as he is proud, and
the presumptive heir of his grandmother,
Lady Frere, stands a good chance of becoming one of the richest men of the day,
and is not a person to be ridiculed, even
were his hands and feet three times the size
that they are.   So Betha tries to be properly
polite to a young gentleman of so much

consequence, the upshot of which is, that
Mr. Frere has already begun to compare her
cousin's boisterous greetings rather unfavour-
ably with the subdued and soft-toned voice
in which she bids him welcome. She looks
so fair and pale as she sits in the lamplight,
with her golden hair bound like a wreath
round her head, that he has fallen more
than once into the bad graces of Mrs. Chapman and her daughter for being caught
gazing at her when he ought to have been
listening to them.

'Now, do talk, Mr. Frere, and make yourself agreeable !' exclaims Blanche, in a lively
manner. 'Tell us all the news. We have
been so cooped up lately, you know, that we
have heard nothing. Where have you been,
and what have you been doing, and what
brings you back again to town so soon? I
thought you had gone down to the Court for
good, until the season commenced. There's
nothing stirring in London, you know; it's
just as dull as ditch-water.'

6—2

'Well, there's less in the country, Miss Chapman. This frost stops all the hunting, and my grandmother is so absurdly particular she won't have any guests at the Court during Lent, so that the house is simply unendurable. How the pater stands it I can't think, but I suppose he has grown used to it by this time.'

'I have always understood that Lady Frere was very reserved, and much addicted to the society of serious people, and so forth,' remarks Aunt Janie; 'but I did not think she was quite so strict as you make her out to be.'

'Oh, she is, Mrs. Chapman, I can assure you—every inch of it. She carries her prejudices to an absurd extent—so far, indeed, that the pater's friends and mine scarcely ever see the inside of the Court. They're none of them good enough for Lady Frere. But it's rather hard upon us, isn't it?'

'Horribly hard!' cries Blanche, laughing. 'I expect you will rather take it out of the old Court when you are master there, Mr. Frere ?'

'That will not be in my father's lifetime,' rejoins Robert Frere, gravely.

'Blanche ! how can you be so heedless ?' interposes Mrs. Chapman. 'It is really sad for you and your dear father, though, Mr. Frere, to be unable to invite whom you like to the Court.'

' It is no home to me in consequence,' returns the young man, simply, 'and never will be, Mrs. Chapman. I often wish my grandmother were more like other women. How jolly some of them can be ! I was dining last night with one of the pleasantest people you ever met—good-looking, clever, and with that happy knack of pleasing everybody alike which so few hostesses possess.'

' Indeed ! what is the name of your paragon ?' demands Mrs. Chapman.

' Mrs. Wallerton !' replies the young man, unhesitatingly.

CHAPTER VII.

' FOR HYACINTH'S SAKE.'

MRS. DURANT died in the middle of December : it is now the middle of March, and during those three months, the name of Wallerton has never passed the lips of either aunt or niece. Not that Mrs. Chapman would have had any objection to discuss the matter, her ideas on this subject, as on several others, having become much modified by time ; but Betha has so visibly shrunk from mentioning either her father or the widow, that Aunt Janie has not had the pluck to take the initiative.

Now as the dreaded name passes so easily and jauntily the lips of Mr. Robert Frere,

the girl's pale face suddenly crimsons : and
she turns her eye imploringly on Mrs. Chapman, as though she asked her dumbly what
to do. Aunt Janie looks a little conscious,
but goes on with her embroidery nevertheless.

'By the way, Miss Durant,' continues Mr.
Frere, with beautiful disregard to the feelings
of his listeners, 'I met a gentleman of your
name there, a Major Durant; is he any
relation ?'

He is surprised to see Betha turn her
head the other way, but Mrs. Chapman
answers the question for her.

'Yes !' she says, gravely ; 'Major Durant
is a relation of my niece, but we have not
seen much of him lately.'

'A most agreeable person,' continues
young Frere, thinking to please ; 'and he
appeared quite at home there. Indeed, I
heard some of the guests suggesting that it
was *une affaire de cœur* between him and
our fair hostess, and I must say it looked like

it. They seemed on the very best of terms, and the major behaved more like the master of the house than a visitor.'

At these words Betha rises suddenly, and with a face working with emotion, runs out of the room.

'Foolish child!' says Aunt Janie with a slight frown, as the closing of the door causes her to look round.

Robert Frere is, of course, all apologies.

'What have I said or done?' he demands with visible distress. 'Have I offended Miss Durant? ought I not to have mentioned the major to her?'

'My dear Mr. Frere, it is not your fault; Betha is foolishly sensitive—that is all! The truth is, Major Durant is her father; but they have, unfortunately, had a little domestic disagreement, and the poor girl is staying with me until it blows over, which I trust it may soon do. These family quarrels are such very unpleasant occurrences. I am

sure we **never had such** a **thing** during poor
dear Dr. Chapman's **life.**'

'But I am so sorry I should have introduced the subject,' urges Mr. Frere. ' Why
did you not caution me, Mrs. Chapman ? I
should **have bitten out my** tongue sooner
than offend Miss Durant.'

' How can you have *offended* **her ?**' interrupts Blanche, pettishly. ' She **hates her
father** and Mrs. Wallerton **too, and I** suppose
she's dreadfully **afraid they'll marry** each
other. But I can't really see what business
it is of hers, and it's all affectation pretending
she cannot bear to hear them spoken of.
But **Betha is** awfully affected.'

' **No, my** darling ! don't say that !' says
Mrs. Chapman, with mild maternal rebuke ;
' the poor girl **is** much to be pitied, though **I**
am not at all sure **if I am right in** encouraging her to keep up this feud **with** her family
any longer. She carries **her** animosity
altogether too far.'

By which speech it will be **seen that Aunt**

Janie is already beginning to weary of the
charge she has taken on herself. The fact is
she cannot help perceiving that Mr. Frere
(who has known her Blanche since childhood)
is more interested in her cousin than he is in
herself; and she foresees shoals and quick-
sands in the sea of matrimony on which she
hopes to launch her only daughter. For
Bobby Frere is also an only child, heir to a
baronetcy and several thousand pounds a
year, and she may look much farther before
she settles Blanche as comfortably as that.
And since Betha's sudden disappearance
causes the young man to become uncom-
municative and *distrait*, and to return to his
chambers much earlier than he has been in
the habit of doing, she speaks more sharply
to her niece on the subject of her conduct
that evening, than she has ever done
before.

'It was not only exceedingly weak and
silly of you, Betha, to leave the room as you
did, when Mr. Frere simply mentioned your

papa's name ; but it was rude and ill-
mannered into the bargain. I really must
say so. You quite spoilt our evening's
enjoyment. Mr. Frere refused to stay for
supper, thinking, I suppose, that I wished to
be upstairs, consoling you ; and so both he
and Blanche were disappointed. I did not
think you would be so selfish !'

'Oh, Aunt Janie ! indeed I did not mean
to upset your evening, but to hear him talk
of papa and—and—her—in that manner—only
three months after—it seemed so shocking. I
felt as if I could not stay and listen to him,'
sobs Betha.

'My dear, you must not be so childish !
It was all very well at first, perhaps, and
I know that I indulged you in it more than I
ought to have done ; but now it is different,
you see. You cannot keep up such feelings
for ever, it would be wicked and unchristian ;
and so the sooner you accustom yourself to
think and talk of your papa as other daughters
do of theirs, the better.'

'Aunt Janie! I can never—*never* do that. He has not been as other fathers are to me! It is impossible to forget the past!'

'Well, my dear, I am sorry to hear you say so, for (for my own part) I confess I am beginning to feel a little tired of these family jars. They are wicked and unnatural, and I am afraid I was very wrong in encouraging you to maintain them.'

'Aunt Janie! are you tired of me?' asks Betha, pointedly.

The scales have suddenly fallen from the girl's eyes. She has been asleep till now, dreaming over her own bereavement and accepting what was given her as freely as she believed that it was offered; but Mrs. Chapman's present manner undeceives her. In a moment she has pierced through the artificial exterior and read the true mind of her aunt beneath it. The enthusiasm has faded; the warmth evaporated; Mrs. Chapman is weary of the *rôle* of benefactress and mother, and feels the charge of her niece to be both burdensome and expensive.

'You are tired of me,' repeats Betha, with kindling eyes.

'Oh no, my dear child! how can you say so?' replies Aunt Janie, looking somewhat foolish notwithstanding; 'but it grieves me terribly to see you so obstinately set against your papa. He is your only parent, you know, Betha; and if anything were to happen to me, what *would* become of you? And as for his dining with Mrs. Wallerton, what non-sense to take umbrage at that! Is the poor man never to have any amusement? He has been moped up for three months now (it has been a most trying time for all of us, as you know, Betha), and if he may not dine out with an old friend——'

'Oh! but, Aunt Janie, you know the reason—you know it so well!'

'I suppose you mean that the news affected you, because you imagine that your papa may take it into his head to marry Mrs. Wallerton.

Well, my dear, you can hardly expect him to remain single for the rest of his life—a man scarcely over forty—it would be ridiculous ; and if he is to marry, I don't see why it should not be Mrs. Wallerton as well as any-one else.   He has only himself to consult in the matter.'

'*Aunt Janie!*' exclaims Betha in a voice of the deepest reproach.

She could not mean more if she used a hundred words to express her meaning.   Her tone demands of her listener if she has for-gotten that agonising scene that took place in the room downstairs when the sight of the woman she so carelessly alludes to drew forth the first words of complaint or accusation that had ever passed the lips of her mother, and which proved to be almost the last words she uttered.

'I know what you would allude to, my dear,' replies Mrs. Chapman, uneasily ; 'but I can only repeat my words : I think this quarrel between yourself and your papa alto-

gether wrong, and I consider it is your duty
to go and ask him to overlook the last three
months and take you back again.'

'*Take me back !*' echoes Betha in a tone of
horror, but the next moment she has closed
her teeth about her upper lip, and resolved
that she will betray no more of her feelings to
one who has evidently lost the power to
sympathise with them. 'Very good, Aunt
Janie,' she adds presently, 'I will think over
what you have said, and try to act upon it.
Good-night. Please leave me to myself, that
I may consider what is the best thing for me
to do.'

'But of course, my dear child,' continues
Aunt Janie, already repenting her words,
'this house is your home as long as ever you
wish to remain in it. Don't think I want to
get rid of you, my darling. You know I
have always said that I look upon you as a
sacred legacy from my beloved sister, and it
is only because I am so afraid that your
future interests may be endangered, that I

even hint at such a thing as a reconciliation between yourself and your dear papa.'

But Aunt Janie's repentance comes a little too late. Betha takes it for what it is worth, and receives it accordingly.

'Yes, yes,' she murmurs faintly, as she turns her head on one side, so as to avoid her aunt's caress. She understands it all now.

' That inhuman monster,' Major Durant, is transformed into her ' dear papa,' and Aunt Janie, who swore she should never return to Northallerton Crescent, has become so anxious concerning her future interests that she thinks it is her duty to go and ask to be taken back again.

' Well, perhaps it *is* my duty,' thinks Betha to herself, as Aunt Janie, having made a feeble, tearful attempt to eat her own words, and found her efforts received with incredulity, has thought it as well to retreat from the field of action; ' it will be a bitter pill to swallow, and I feel as if I would rather sweep a crossing than go through with

it; but for Hyacinth's sake, and for what
darling mother said about her, I think I can
do it—at all events I will try. And if anything should happen to prevent it—if papa
should hold to his determination not to receive me again—why, then I will earn my
bread by teaching, or sewing, or any means,
sooner than return here. I could have lived
with Aunt Janie for ever, so long as I
believed she loved me; but now—now it is
very different,' thinks Betha, with proud, in-
dignant tears flashing in her lovely grey eyes.

She says *if* her father should hold to his
determination; but in her own heart she has
little doubt of the issue of her appeal. She
appreciates how exquisitely painful it will be
for her to make it; how humbling to her
pride; what a sacrilegious trampling down of
all her most sacred memories! She knows
that if she returns to Northallerton Crescent,
she will have daily to see and hear things
that will wound and torture her; but she says
she can do it and bear it, and she *will* do it

and bear it, for Hyacinth's sake. But that
Major Durant should seriously reject her
overtures for a reconciliation does not enter
into her calculations. A father determinately
stand out against his own child! Why, the
thing is almost an anomaly! for what do we
not forgive our children? Not only for
youthful faults, impetuous answers, and careless disobedience, but for many graver things;
for ingratitude, rebellion, forgetfulness, or even
for deceit or robbery. There is *nothing* for
which a parent finds it impossible to pardon
his child, till Death closes the account of love
between them.

But many fathers have so refused to forgive the errors of their offspring. No, not
fathers, but brutes! Brutes not worthy the
name of men or parents! And with all
Betha's experience of Major Durant's unkind
treatment of her mother, she is not prepared
to believe he will carry his resentment
beyond her grave. She is still very young,
poor child; she has seen but little of the world

and its ways, and she knows nothing of how
passion will influence a man to act against his
best interests. She dresses herself with
trembling fingers the next morning, and prepares to find her way back to Northallerton
Crescent. She does not tell Mrs. Chapman
of the mission on which she is bound; Aunt
Janie may think she is going for her usual
morning walk, for a barrier has risen up
between the two since the evening before,
although the elder woman does her best to
cover it by honeyed smiles and kisses.

The weather is still very keen and frosty;
but it is not cold enough to make Betha
shiver as she does under her fur, as she comes
in view of the familiar row of houses. A
dozen times she paces backwards and forwards
in front of the hall-door before she can
summon up the courage to ring the bell, in
hopes perhaps of seeing a face at the window
that shall nod or smile or beckon to her and
give her the encouragement she needs to
enter.

But there is no sign of any living creature about the place, and at last the girl, calling up all her resolution, runs up the steps and demands admittance. A stranger opens the door to her, and she is just about to inquire for her father, when she catches sight of Hyacinth in the hall; Hyacinth, the imp who will always hang about the banisters and stairs against all orders to the contrary. The appearance of her little sister opens the floodgates of Betha's emotion. Her first thought is, how she could ever have remained away from her so long.

'Cinthy! Cinthy darling!' she cries lovingly, as she presses forward to clasp her in her arms.

But the child draws backward—hardly seeming to recognise her sister in those black robes, and with so pale and thin a face.

'Are you Betha?' she inquires wonderingly.

'Yes, darling! your own sister Betha.

Don't you know me, Cinthy? Oh, I have so longed and longed to see you!'

'Oh yes! I know you of course,' says Miss Pert; 'but I mustn't speak to you. My papa has expressly forbidden it. He says we are never to speak to each other again—never!'

'He cannot be so cruel!' exclaims Betha, impetuously. 'He would not prevent my speaking to my own mother's child! Dear, dear mother, you haven't forgotten her yet, have you, Cinthy? You haven't forgotten our blessed mother in heaven, who is thinking of you, and loving you every day?'

'Of course I have not forgotten her, Betha. How could I, in only three months?' replies the young lady, with an assumption of superiority. 'Bentham took me to see her grave several times. But oh, Betha, I've got such a lovely new doll! I wish I could show it you!'

'So you shall, darling. Where is dear old Bentham?' says Betha, forgetting everything but that she is amongst familiar faces again.

'Here I am, my dear Miss Betha!' exclaims the nurse, coming downstairs, and throwing her arms about Betha's neck. 'I heard your voice right up to the nursery—it's just the moral of your blessed mamma's : I was sure it could be no one but you. But oh, my dear, what brings you here ? Suppose the major should come home and find you ? Aren't you afraid to risk it ?'

'No, dear nurse ! No ! I have come for the express purpose of speaking to him ; and if he is out, I shall wait till he returns. I have come to tell him I will return home again, Bentham, and to ask him to let things be as they were before. Oh, I can't think how it is I have stayed away so long from you and Cinthy !'

' Poor dear,' says Bentham, sympathisingly, 'you've been nearly off your head, I dare say, with your trouble. And I'd have been over to see you, Miss Betha, but he wouldn't let me. The major's laid his commands upon every one of us, as we wasn't ever to speak to you.'

'But it will be all right again now, nurse.'

'I hope it will, my dear, I'm sure, for we've had a sad time of it. And I've missed you sorely, Miss Betha, that I have.'

'And I wanted you to see my doll,' cries Hyacinth; 'it's such a beauty, with blue eyes, and yellow hair, and a red satin frock. Mrs. Wallerton brought it from Paris with her. And Mrs. Wallerton buys me my dresses now, and my hats, and I'm going to live with her some day. Papa says so!'

'*What!*' exclaims Betha, with one hand pressed upon her heart.

'Lor! my dear, if you're going to start like that every time Mrs. Wallerton is named in this house, you had better bide where you are,' says the servant. 'Why, she rules the roost here, and orders me and Miss Cinthy about like anything.'

'But she is very kind,' interposes Cinthy,

eagerly; 'she gave me my doll, and lots of sugar-plums, and I *like* her, awfully !'

Betha draws away from her little sister with a sudden pang. It is true, then ! Her suspicions are correct. Mrs. Wallerton will doubtless, before long, rule altogether at Northallerton Crescent ! Will she ever be able to bear it ?

The question is soon answered. At that moment the latch-key is turned in the door, and Major Durant enters the hall. Betha turns to confront her father. As he recognises her, he frowns deeply, and addresses Bentham.

'What is this ? Have I not given you express orders that this—this *person* is not to be admitted within my walls ?'

'Papa, papa ! it is I—it is Betha.'

But Major Durant takes no notice of the appeal.

'What do you mean by disobeying me ?' he shouts to Bentham.

'I didn't let Miss Durant in, sir ! I

heard her talking to Miss Hyacinth in the hall, and I just came down to listen, not five minutes ago. I didn't think there could be any harm in that, sir.'

'My orders to you were, that no communication of any sort was to take place between yourself and Miss Hyacinth and this—this person! under penalty of receiving your dismissal from my service. You have disobeyed me, and you must go. Take your month's warning from this date!'

'Oh, sir! pray don't send me away! Think how long I have been in your service —with these two dear children from their birth, and with the poor mistress through all her illness. I have served you faithfully for many years, sir! Pray don't part me from Miss Cinthy now; it'll just go to break my heart.'

'You have wilfully disobeyed me, and you must leave. Let us have no more words on the subject!' replies Major Durant, preparing to pass into the dining-room.

'Father! are you not going to speak to me?' exclaims Betha, as she places herself in his way.

'No! I have nothing to say to you. The sooner you return to your aunt's house the better!'

'Oh, papa! I cannot return there—not to live! I came here to-day to ask you to let me come home again! I dare say I was wrong and hasty to act as I did, but I was in great trouble and I hardly knew what to do or say! I loved my mother very *very* dearly, papa! You know that, and you will not count it to me as a fault, I am sure!'

If Betha thinks the allusion to her mother will soften her father's heart towards her, she is very much mistaken, for with it comes the remembrance of how she slighted Mrs. Wallerton for that mother's sake. And she looks too much like the dead woman as she stands there, with pallid cheeks and swollen eyes and quivering lips—too much as *she* used to appear when she pleaded against her husband's cruelty in preferring her false and smooth-tongued friend to herself.

When a man is attempting to stamp out such unpleasant recollections by drinking deep at the fountain of a new love, he does not care to have a living reminder of his frailty, as it were, constantly before him; and as his fair-haired daughter raises her mother's eyes to his face and pleads to him in her mother's voice, he positively *hates* her.

'I never blamed you for loving your late mother,' he answers coldly; 'I blamed you for the method you took of showing that love. However, it is futile to discuss the subject. You have chosen your lot, and you must abide by it!'

'But, papa! surely you will not refuse to receive me again, if I am willing to come! I will try and do my duty, papa! I will say that I am sorry for what has occurred, and I will be as good a daughter to you as I possibly can, for my dear mother's sake.'

'I am much obliged for all your good intentions, but as far as I am concerned they are useless. Your conduct has closed these doors against you for ever.'

'Do you mean to say that we are never to be reconciled again?' cries Betha aghast as a true sense of the position she has placed herself in dawns upon her mind. 'But I have nowhere to go, papa! Aunt Janie is tired of keeping me; and if you turn me out of doors again, I must beg in the streets, or starve.'

Major Durant's face assumes an expression of malicious triumph.

'I foresaw what all your fine independent speeches would result in,' he says, with a fiendish smile, 'but I am not to be taken in by them a second time. You have received a first-rate education, and if Mrs. Chapman refuses to keep you in idleness any longer, you had better turn it to some account. You are a *woman*, remember—sixteen on your last birthday, and amenable to the discipline of no one. If the law compels me to allow you a pittance I will do so, but not in this house nor under any roof that shelters me and my belongings. You have chosen to leave it once of your own accord, you will be good enough to leave it now on my orders ; and if you attempt to enter it again, I shall put the matter into the hands of the law!'

All the pride in Elizabeth Durant's nature is boiling on the surface. Her father's words and manner have decided her. She would not stoop to ask another favour at his hands now, if she had to die without it.

'You are right!' she answers slowly, and with a look of ineffable scorn ; 'the same roof can never shelter you and me again. I *can* support myself, papa!—and I will. And if I fail, I will die sooner than eat a crust of bread that has been paid for with your money. Good-bye, darling Cinthy! Don't forget poor Betha, and mother in heaven; and remember we shall all meet there some day soon!'

'I wish you wouldn't make me cry! It's

disagreeable of you,' says Cinthy, whining.
'And don't go, Betha, till you've seen my doll!'

'Good-bye, dear old Bentham! Take
double care of Cinthy, for J shall never be a
trouble to you again!'

'Oh, my dear blessed child, let me kiss
you once more before you go!'

'If you presume to fly in my face by such
an action,' exclaims Major Durant, fiercely,
'you shall not even remain here till your
month is up, but leave the house at the same
moment as herself!'

'Bentham! you must not—you shall not!'
cries Betha, as she keeps off the old servant
with one hand. 'No one must suffer for
this business but myself. I am going, papa;
there is no need to thrust me from your doors,
and I will never re-enter them, until you ask
me to do so.'

'Then you will stay out of them for ever,'
says the major, as the hall-door slams on the
figure of his eldest child.

CHAPTER VIII.

'I WILL ALWAYS BE YOUR FRIEND.'

MR. ROBERT FRERE is standing in the little drawing-room of Mrs. Chapman's house, gazing thoughtfully from the window, and wondering when the ladies will return. He arrived there, half an hour before, with his hands full of Russian violets, very anxious to make amends for the awkwardness which had broken up the party on the previous evening—and still more anxious (if the truth must be told) to see Betha again, and learn from her manner if she bears him any ill-will for that unlucky *lapsus linguæ* that drove her from the room. But Aunt Janie and Blanche left the house soon after Betha, and Bobby's only alternative is to lounge about on chair after chair in the small drawing-room, until one or all of them shall see fit to return. As he does so, if he looks eminently ugly, he also looks eminently gentlemanly.

Lady Frere would resent the idea of his even looking ugly. Large noses and mouths have been the leading characteristics of the Freres for generations past, and Bobby would scarcely be recognised by his grand-mother unless he perpetuated the family features with the family blood. She is as proud of one as of the other. She thinks there are no men equal to the Freres, and no women really worthy of being mated with them.

Bobby, though strictly reared in the faith of his forefathers, and rather proud of his big nose, perhaps as a mark of his blood, still credits himself with all the ugliness he pos-sesses, and is very humble on the score of his own attractions. He is a young man,

now two or three and twenty, but he is still
as awkward and uncouth as when he was
sixteen, and just as apt to upset a table of
ornaments, or spill a cup of tea over a lady's
dress, as he was then. Of good birth and
position, with plenty of money to throw
about, it is not likely that his big nose has
stood in the way of his fortunes with the fair
sex ; but since he recovered from his calf-
love, Bobby Frere has never seen any girl
who really enchained his interest, until he
met with Elizabeth Durant. He is clever
and practical, as most ugly men are, and there
is something in the flashes he has caught of
Betha's spirit that have appealed to his
own.

He has the power to read beneath the girl's
half-awakened intellect, a genius that rightly
directed may stir the world ; and he has taken
it into his head that he has a divine mission
to encourage and direct it. In those quiet
evenings they have spent together at Mrs.
Chapman's, he has discovered how much

Betha has both read and retained ; how
many bright clever thoughts pass through
her active brain ; how imitative she is ; how
witty, how quick at repartee. It is only a
sentence here and there dropped in general
conversation that has led him to the convic-
tion ; and it is only a glance here and there,
sometimes pathetic and sometimes gay, that
has made him believe that Betha is not only
the cleverest but the most charming girl he
has ever seen.

How astonished will be the forlorn young
heart and aching breast that are hurrying
towards him as he ruminated to learn such
an astounding truth.

Mr. Frere hears the handle of the front
door turn, and immediately rises to receive
his coming hostess. But Mrs. Chapman
does not appear. A pale face is thrust
inside the drawing-room door instead, and
instantly withdrawn again, but not before he
has caught sight of it.

' Miss Durant !' he exclaims joyfully ; and

then Betha is compelled to enter and be
ordinarily polite to him.

'How do you do, Mr. Frere? I thought
Aunt Janie was here. Have you been long
alone?'

'No—yes—that is, about half an hour;
but I would have waited the whole day for
the pleasure of seeing you. Do you feel the
cold, Miss Durant? you are looking so pale
—I thought it was thawing this morning, as
I walked over here.'

'I think it *is* thawing,' replies Betha, as
she bends over the fire. 'Oh, what lovely
violets!'

(Is there a woman in the world who can
resist flowers?)

'I brought them for you. Will you do
me the honour of accepting them?' says
Bobby Frere with much needless stammer-
ing, as he thrusts the bouquet into her hands.

'For me! did you really? How very, *very*
kind of you!' replies Betha, gratefully; but
there is no ring of pleasure in her voice.

'Yes, I was so anxious to see you, Miss Durant, and apologise for my stupid blunder last evening. I didn't know, of course—I had not heard, you see—and—and (don't be angry with me for mentioning it again); but I would have cut off my right hand sooner than give you pain—indeed I would.'

'It is nothing! Pray, say no more about it, Mr. Frere,' replies Betha, quickly. 'I was foolish and thoughtless; but I have got over that now.'

She seems so unlike the girl who flew out of the room last night with flashing eyes and crimsoned cheeks, that Mr. Frere can only stare at her, and wonder what can have happened between that time and this, to render her so self-possessed and calm.

'Then I may consider myself forgiven?' he says.

'Quite forgiven. The subject is not one I should choose, but I will never resent the mention of it again.'

'Ah, Miss Durant, how good you are!

You make me bold enough to say, how glad
I should be if I could render you any assistance. If there were only one thing in which
I could help you, or be of service to you, I
should be so very, very happy !'

'Perhaps you *can* help me,' says Betha,
with her eyes fixed dreamily upon the
fire.

'Tell me in what way.'

'Why, you are rich, Aunt Janie says, and
have plenty of friends ; and I want so much
to make money, Mr. Frere. Get me something to do—some work—some employment,
and it will be the greatest favour you could
show me.'

'Work — employment !' echoes Bobby ;
'you are laughing at me, Miss Durant.'

It appears so incredible to those who have
been accustomed to every luxury from their
birth that young people — and especially
young women—should be called upon to
labour for their daily bread.

'I am not laughing,' replies Betha, gravely ;

'I have no home, and I am going to work for my living.'

'No home! when you live here with Mrs. Chapman!'

'Oh no! I don't,' rejoins the girl, quickly; 'I am only staying here on a visit, and I shall soon be gone.'

'But your father, Major Durant — you said I might mention him, you know, Betha —what would he say to the idea of your taking up employment like any common person?'

'*My father, Major Durant,*' repeats Betha, with an hysterical laugh. 'It is he that told me to do it. I have just come from him, Mr. Frere, and he turned me out of his house and told me I might beg or starve before he would admit me there again. Oh, I ought not to tell you of these things, perhaps, but all the world will know it soon. And so you see, I *must* work—I must get some honest work to do; and if you can tell me of any plan by which I can turn what knowledge I have to account, I shall be so very grateful to you!'

But Mr. Frere can only stand there silent and aghast at the reception of her news. Those hands to work—that golden-crowned head to be bowed over her daily toil—those sweet grey eyes to be dimmed by midnight study! Oh, the thought alone is sacrilege! The girl must either have made some hideous mistake, or the father been playing on her feelings with a view to testing her courage and determination.

'Good heavens!' he murmurs; 'it cannot be true.'

'But it *is* true, Mr. Frere—and please don't begin to pity me, because I must think and act for myself, and there will be plenty of time for sentiment afterwards.' Then she turns and looks at him, and the childishness of her nature appeals to the youth of his. The elder people are all against her; perhaps this boy will accept her confidence and understand her feelings and respect them. 'It is all on account of mother, you know,' she whispers, with a great sob in her throat. 'I cannot forget her, and—and—papa can, and so it is best we should not live together. Don't ask me any more, please, but if you *can* help me I shall think you are a true friend, and I shall never forget it.'

'I could live and die for you!' cries Bobby Frere, impulsively; and then the great secret comes out: 'Betha, darling! let me live for you. I know we are both very young, and perhaps the pater would want us to wait for a little— at least, I don't think the pater would, but grandmamma's so very particular, and she leads him by the nose. Anyway, you could stay here with your aunt until they gave their consent; and I'm such an idle fellow, you know, I could see you as often as ever I liked, and——'

'Stay here! stay *here!*' repeats Betha, in a bewildered manner; 'but I have just told you I must go, Mr. Frere. I am going out into the world to make my own living—

there is nothing to be done by staying here !'

‘You don't understand me, darling — I mean that you should only remain here until we are married.'

‘*Married !*’ says Betha — ‘you and I *married !*’

She is a woman in many things, but she is a perfect child in this. Not only has she been so securely guarded beneath her mother's wing that no man has ever approached her near enough to make such a suggestion, but she has lived so much at home in the companionship of Mrs. Durant and her little sister, that she has not been in the habit of discussing the subject even with her female friends. And as to imagining it could be proposed to her so soon, and from the lips of Mr. Frere—the idea frightens as much as it surprises her.

‘Why not ?' demands Bobby, gaining courage to draw nearer and take her hand in his. ‘If you will promise to be my wife,

Betha, all your troubles will be over, and you need never talk again about such a dreadful thing as working for your liveli-hood.'

But Betha wrenches her hand out of his, and retreats to the further end of the hearth-rug with a face of crimson.

'Oh, no, no ! you mustn't talk to me like that—you have made a great mistake.   You are altogether wrong !' she exclaims vehe-mently.

'Don't you love me,' cries Bobby—'not a little bit ?'

'Not the least bit !   I never did, and I never shall.   Oh, I wish I had never told you anything if it is to end like this !'

'Don't say that, Betha, because it pains me so.   I wanted to help you—indeed I did: but all of a sudden it flashed upon my mind how much I love you—and I thought you might consent to be my wife, instead.   I know I'm an ugly fellow, and have very little to recommend me, but I have never loved anybody before, Betha, and I shall never love anybody again—at least, not in that way !'

' Oh, why did you say anything about the other thing,' says Betha, relenting at the pathetic appeal of those soft brown eyes, ' and when I so much want a friend ?'

' Let me be your friend still ! If you are really bent upon this plan I will go to the Duchess of Somerton and Lady Milverton, and see if they can think of some work that is fit for you to do. I know lots of old ladies who would be delighted to help you !'

' No, no !' says Betha, with a mournful shake of the head ; ' I think you had better leave it alone, Mr. Frere. I must work, but I do not wish to get mixed up with all those grand people, who will know papa's name and find out my whole history !'

The pride of blood is rising in Betha again, and she regrets she has ever mentioned the matter to her companion.

' I must go now,' she says presently, for

she is longing to get away from the pleading
look he keeps fixed upon her, 'but I dare say
Aunt Janie and Blanche will soon be home.
Good-bye, Mr. Frere.'   .

'Good-bye,' he says hoarsely, as he holds
the hand she tenders him ; 'and is there *no*
hope, Betha ?'

'I will always be your friend,' replies the
girl gravely, as she turns from him and quits
the room.

CHAPTER IX.

'I AM BETTER NOW.'

BETHA runs up to her own room and remains there in the cold, half frightened and bewildered. There is none of the elation about her that most young girls feel on first receiving a proposal of marriage. She thinks a fresh misfortune has occurred to her, and wonders if she is to blame, or what she has done to bring about so unfortunate a mistake on Mr. Frere's part. She tries to find out if the error is on her side, and if that great mysterious thing called love has really come upon her unawares; and to that end pictures herself walking to church with Bobby Frere, and looking up at his uncouth face and

figure, whilst a crowd of spectators are gazing
at them. And, young as she is, the girl
knows by the shudder that comes over her at
the mere idea, that the young man has placed
a gulf between them by what he has said
that day, that no time perhaps will have the
power to bridge over. She listens to his
heavy step pacing the little room below for
some minutes after she has left it, and then
she hears him go downstairs and pass out
into the road, slamming the hall-door after
him. That sound is the greatest relief Betha
can experience, and dressed in her walking-
things, she sits upon her bed trying to think
to whom she can next apply for assistance in
her undertaking. As she does so, the
thought of Miss Denny comes into her mind.
The lady superintendent of Princess College
has considered Miss Durant's energy and
determination of character to be less
'elegant' than her own lowered eyelids and
minced words approve of; but, at the same
time, she has always acknowledged her ability

and lamented it was to be thrown away in
private life. Betha thinks Miss Denny
would not refuse to give her a trial as a pupil
teacher perhaps, or to assist with the junior
classes for languages and elocution. The
idea is as hateful to the girl as it can possibly
be—she knows that she would rather scrub
floors than drum accent, and emphasis, and
gesture into soulless ears, but the instinct of
race is strong in her, and she feels that she
must not attempt physical work until she
has failed with the intellectual. She is
roused from her reverie by the voices of her
aunt and cousin as they toil up the narrow
staircase to their bedroom, which is next to
hers.

'Mamma! I think it is disgraceful,' says
Blanche, petulantly; 'Mary says she was for
a whole hour cooped up with Bobby Frere in
the drawing-room. She is under your care
now, and you ought to teach her better!'

'I begin to wish she had never been under
my care,' sighs Aunt Janie; 'what with

your disagreements and Major Durant's ob-
duracy and the way people talk, I'm pretty
nearly sick of the whole affair. And she's
such an expense, too. The bills have been
half again as much since she entered the
house!'

'Of course they have! Mary takes advantage of there being an extra mouth to eat
double on her own account, and she is always
complaining of the increased trouble into the
bargain. But, mamma, you must speak to
Betha about Bobby Frere. I won't have her
take my friends away in that fashion. I've
seen her trying to do it for weeks past.'

'Oh dear! oh dear!' laments Mrs. Chapman, weakly; 'I do wish I could see an end
to it. I little thought when I sheltered her
from her father's anger what I was bringing
on myself. If nothing happens during the
next few days, I must really go and speak to
Major Durant on the subject.'

Betha's indignation, as she overhears this
conversation, reaches boiling-point. Her

impulse is to rush out upon the landing and
tell her cousin and her aunt that, very far
from wishing to take their friend Mr. Frere
from them, she has just refused his overtures
of a much more tender nature. But her in-
born delicacy, joined to a recollection of the
pleading look in those soft brown eyes,
prevents Betha from defending herself at his
expense. Aunt Janie and Blanche must
think what they choose : their words have
only made her more determined to take the
first opportunity of seeing Miss Denny, and
try to relieve them of her unwelcome presence.

But at that juncture a loud double knock
is heard, and in another minute Mary taps at
Betha's door to say that Miss Kemyss is
waiting below to see her.

Betha runs down at once to greet her
friend.

Mattie Kemyss has been a constant visitor
at Mrs. Chapman's house during Betha's
sojourn there, and has more than once

pressed her old schoolfellow to pay her a
lengthened visit.   Mattie is the only daughter
of a rich widower, who indulges her in every
whim, so long as she allows him to pursue his
own pleasures unmolested, so that the beautiful girl is ostensibly her own mistress, and
now that she has given up the Princess
College, holds high revels at Albert Gate.

'Dear, darling Betha! I am so delighted
to see you,' she cries, in her pretty, silly
enthusiasm, as she devours her friend with
kisses; 'I have been dying to come over for
the last week, but I had such a horrid cold
the doctor wouldn't hear of my going out.
But I've come to steal you away, Betha.
Now, no excuses, for I won't take any;
we've got something going on at home, and
we can't possibly do without you!'

'What is it, dear Mattie?'

'Well, it will be my birthday on the 3rd
of April, and Conrad Levison (that's the
fellow I am engaged to, you know) has set
his heart upon our getting up some private

theatricals or tableaux vivants, or something
of that sort, and you must come and arrange
them for us and teach us all our parts.'

'I, Mattie?' says Betha, with surprise;
'but what do I know about theatricals?'

'Oh, my dear child! don't talk such nonsense. Just think of the heaps of plays you
used to spout from at college, and Mr.
Lillingstone always declared you were a born
actress. I know you can put us right in the expression and feature and everything. Besides
which,' continues Mattie, caressingly, 'you
must come, for my sake. You can't think
how I long to have you to stay with me,
Betha. I am so lonely in that big house,
with papa and my brothers always away.
Why, sometimes I hardly see them for days
together. And papa is so anxious for you to
come, too. See! I have brought you a note
from him, and he says if you will consent to
stay a month or two with me, you will place
him under the greatest obligation.'

A month or two at Albert Gate! An immediate release from the grudging hospitality of Aunt Janie, and time to think over and mature her own plans. The offer is too good to be rejected. Betha accepts it eagerly.

'Oh, Mattie, it is very good of you to want me, and I should like to come. It will seem like the old days to be talking to you again. And I have much to tell you, dear— much that will surprise and shock you, perhaps, for I—I am not very happy here.'

'My poor darling!' cries the affectionate Mattie, as she throws her arms about Betha; 'don't think or speak of it again. Let us go at once. My carriage is waiting at the door, and I told papa that I should, if possible, take you back with me.'

'You must give me time to tell my aunt,' replies Betha, as she leaves the apartment. The next minute she is standing on the threshold of Mrs. Chapman's room.

'Aunt Janie! Mr. Kemyss has been kind enough to send me an invitation to stay with

Mattie for a few weeks, and I am going back with her at once.’

There is a new look in Betha’s face that Aunt Janie does not quite like, and she affects to be much astonished at her news.

‘ Going back with Miss Kemyss at once ! Well, really, Betha, I think, considering the hospitality you have received under my roof, that you might have paid me the compliment of consulting my wishes first.’

‘ I will not go unless you wish me to do so, Aunt Janie ; but from what you said last night, I thought it would be rather a relief to you than otherwise.’

Mrs. Chapman grows very red.

‘ Of course I do not wish to deprive you of any enjoyment, my dear, but your announcement is rather sudden. What do you wish done about your boxes ?’

‘ Will you be so good as to send them after me to Albert Gate—*all* of them, please, Aunt Janie, as my visit may be a long one.’

‘ One would really think you intended run-

ning away from us for good,' says Aunt
Janie, nervously.

The girl does not answer, but she looks her
in the face, quietly, earnestly, fully, and the
pale blue eyes sink before the grey ones.

'Whatever may be in the future, Aunt
Janie, I thank you very much for what is
past. I dare say I have been a somewhat
troublesome visitor. A great grief is so apt
to make one selfish; but I am getting better
now, and I mean to work more and occupy
my mind. Good-bye! I shall write to you
often, and tell you what I am doing; and I
shall always feel very grateful to you for the
kindness you have shown me, and sorry that
I should have brought any worry or expense
upon you.'

'Oh, my darling child! whoever said that
you were any worry or expense to me?' replies Aunt Janie, weeping. 'The few words
I let drop last night were only intended for
your good.'

She guesses now that the girl does not

mean to return to her, and though it is the
end she has been hoping for, she is too weak-
minded to rejoice that it has come.

'I believe that—or I believe that you believe it,' says truthful Betha; 'but let us
never think or speak of it again. Good-bye
to you both. When I have been a few days
in Albert Gate I shall be better able to write
and tell you all I think and feel than I am
to say it.' And in a few minutes she is roll-
ing away with Mattie Kemyss to her new
abode.

Betha has not been happy whilst with
Mrs. Chapman. During the last few days
she has been wounded and outraged. Still,
she cannot help feeling, as she drives from
Earl's Court, that the last mooring has been
cut, to send her little boat adrift on the path-
less sea of life.

CHAPTER X.

'IT IS IMPOSSIBLE!'

MR. KEMYSS is a merchant, and a Jew, though it is very seldom he can be brought to acknowledge the fact. Both he and his children bear the traces in their features of Hebraic origin—shown forth in the lovely Mattie only by the languid softness of her dark eyes, and the delicate shape of her aquiline nose — but they have all been brought up to ignore the circumstance. They associate with the men and women of their own nation, Mr. Conrad Levison, to whom Miss Kemyss is engaged to be married, being one of the richest and best-known diamond-merchants in the City. But they do not attend the Synagogue, nor perform any of the rites of their supposed religion. Mr. Kemyss, indeed, professes (if he professes anything) to be a Freethinker. His sons, who are both engaged in the same trade with himself, are as careless as most young men of the present day; and the daughter of the house is allowed to do exactly as she chooses in all things, no limit being placed on her expenditure, nor supervision directed to her mind—the worst possible training for a young, heedless creature, with extraordinary beauty, an affectionate heart, and a very small amount of brains.

The house at Albert Gate is large, and handsomely furnished, replete with every luxury, and provided with an ample retinue of servants. As the two girls leave the carriage and pass into the library, their feet sink into a velvet-pile carpet, their senses are saluted by the odours of choice flowers, and their glances fall on walls covered with some of the best specimens of modern art.

Elizabeth Durant has not been accustomed to such a palatial residence as this, but nothing that she sees startles her. Her father's house in Northallerton Crescent contains most of the comforts of a middle-class residence : her Aunt Janie's, in Earl's Court, rather less : yet you might place the girl in a mansion twice as magnificent as that of Mr. Kemyss without making her heart beat faster by a single stroke. It forms one of the greatest distinctions between the well-born man, or woman, and the child of the soil. You may raise the former to the pinnacle of a throne without making him giddy ; he feels himself so capable of filling any position in life, that no elevation dazzles him : and he sinks as gracefully as he can rise.

As Betha and Mattie ensconce themselves by the library fire until afternoon tea shall be served to them, the one girl lets her glances rove over the luxurious apartment they sit in as carelessly as the other ; each is intent only on interesting herself in the affairs of her companion.

' And so you are engaged to be married, Mattie ?' says Betha. ' How wonderful that seems, when one remembers that only three months ago we were trying for the same prizes.'

' And that you got them all,' laughs Mattie. ' Well, I can't say I see anything very wonderful in it myself, Betha ! It only strikes me as disagreeable and inconvenient. I can't tell you how I hate the whole business.'

' Hate being engaged !' exclaims Betha, with wide-open eyes.

Her knowledge of love and marriage has been culled from the pages of poets and novelists, and she has thought, hitherto, that when a girl became engaged she had reached the very acme of happiness.

' Indeed I do,' replies Mattie. ' You can't imagine what a bore it is. The creature expects one to be always at his beck and call ;

and if I break an appointment with him, or go to a party when he has arranged to take me to the theatre, he calls on papa for an explanation, and then there are black looks, and I am called to order, and Mr. Levison sulks and doesn't come near us for a week, which is the best thing he ever does.'

'But don't you like going out with him then?' asks Betha.

'*Like it,* my dear!—I should think not! He is only thirty, or thereabouts, but he's the most awful old fogey you ever saw. He won't take me anywhere but behind the curtain of a private box, nor let me dance round dances, and he makes a fuss if I wear a low dress; and if I happen to nod to any young fellow I meet, why, I don't hear the end of it for a month. Oh, I hate him like poison! and if I don't lead him a dance when we're married, it will be a pity, I can tell you!'

'But, Mattie! surely you will never marry him—not if you hate him,' gasps Betha, her breath quite taken away by the revelations of her friend; 'why should you do it, dear, unless you wish it with your whole heart?'

'Why should I do it, Betha? Because he's one of the richest men in England. Have you never heard of the Levisons? Papa says they're a money power in the City, and I'm to have a couple of thousand a year for pin-money alone. Oh! I *do* wish it, I assure you—I wouldn't have the match broken off for the world; but I mean to go my own way, nevertheless. I couldn't do anything else with Conrad Levison; for in the first place we have not two ideas in common—you will die of laughing when you hear what a prig he is —and in the second, he's such an out-and-out Jew: and I hate Jews!'

Betha is too polite to suggest that her friend has every reason not to hate the people she speaks of. She is so amazed at and sorry for what she has heard, that she can only stare in the fire, and wonder silently how such a marriage can possibly lead to anything but misery.

'You haven't got any little affair of this sort on hand yourself, have you, Betha?' demands Mattie presently, as she sips the tea from her delicate porcelain cup.

'Oh no! How should I?' says Betha, colouring. 'I—I—never see anybody, and I have hardly been out of the house, you know. Besides, my lot will be a very different one from yours, Mattie, though it may not be less happy. I told you I had many things to say to you. One is, that when I leave your house it will be to earn my own living.'

And then she tells her friend, in confidence, what has been already told for her; and Mattie embraces her warmly, and declares that as long as she lives Betha must share her money and her home.

'You dear, sweet darling!' she cries. 'Fancy your working for your daily bread in any way whilst I have two thousand a year for my pin-money! But I will give half of it to you, Betha. A thousand pounds will keep you very comfortable till you are married yourself, which you may be before you leave this house, after all.'

But Betha shakes her head and smiles. She is so much older in mind and feeling than her friend.

'It is just like your generous self, Mattie, to think of such a thing. But it is quite impossible, dear; and if you had fifty thousand a year that you did not know what to do with, it would make no difference. I would not accept five shillings when I could earn them. I feel very keenly on this point, Mattie. I think that pride is the strongest feeling I possess, and I must beg you not to mention a word of what I have told you to Mr. Kemyss, for fear he might offer to assist me. If he wants to do so, I should leave the house at once. And I think I shall be so happy here. I'm sure you won't drive me from it.'

'Oh dear, oh dear! this is very uncomfortable,' sighs Mattie. 'I shall begin to hate the sight of money, if it's never to do any good. But we mustn't begin to mope, Betha, must we? Let us talk about the theatricals.'

'By all means,' says Betha, brightening up. 'Where are they to be held?'

'In the back drawing-room. We have a stage and footlights all ready, but we can't agree what to do. I want tableaux, but Mr. Levison is trying to persuade papa to have a play, just because he fancies he can act, and knows he is too hideous for anything else. I told him we would appear together as "Beauty and the Beast," but he didn't seem to relish the idea.'

'I am afraid you must try his patience, Mattie; and to act a play will certainly be a much greater exercise of brain.'

'When you know I haven't got any,' says Miss Kemyss, who is never backward in acknowledging her own deficiencies.

'Oh, Mattie, you don't do yourself justice. There are many little drawing-room pieces in which you might appear with the greatest advantage.'

'Well, it strikes me the less I open my mouth the better. That is why I want to have tableaux. I know I can look nice if I can't do anything else. But you will act too —won't you, Betha? Nothing will go off properly unless you take a part in it.'

But at this proposal Betha shakes her head resolutely.

'No, no, Mattie! You mustn't ask me. Remember how deep my mourning is yet. It would not be proper that I should do so, and entirely against my own inclinations.'

Her friend continues to urge her, but in vain. Betha promises to take any amount of trouble that may be necessary for the preparation of the approaching performance, but she positively declines to appear herself. When Mr. Kemyss meets her, later in the evening, he welcomes her very kindly to his house, begging her to remain there as long as ever her aunt will give her permission to stay. The brothers also—Lionel and Alfred Kemyss—pay her so much attention that she is subjected to a merciless amount of 'chaff' from Mattie.

But though Betha dislikes the chaff, she is grateful for the attention which makes her feel thoroughly at home. Indeed, in a few days the family seem to have established her at Albert Gate as one of themselves, and it becomes quite strange to the girl to wake up with a start and remember that in a very short time she must go forth again to seek the work by which she hopes to maintain herself.

There is one of the circle at Albert Gate, though, whom Betha cannot like, though she is anxious to do so, and that is Mr. Conrad Levison, Mattie's affianced husband : a short ill-made man, with a head like a barber's block, and a look of sinister coldness, Mr. Levison can certainly have nothing but his money to recommend him. He does not appear to be fond of Miss Kemyss—few men perhaps could be fond of a silly girl who seizes every opportunity to irritate or contradict them—but yet he is profoundly jealous of her. He follows her movements about the room as a cat watches a mouse, and is ready to take offence at the least slight she puts upon him. And Betha, ignorant as she is of such matters, yet knows sufficient to tremble for the happiness of her friend, linked for life to such a man.

Mattie gains her own way with respect to the tableaux vivants, and decides to appear in the triple characters of the 'Sleeping Beauty,' 'Lady Jane Grey,' and 'Titania,' which puts it out of all question that Mr. Levison should assist her either as the Fairy Prince, Lord Dudley, or Oberon. To uphold these parts, the services of a young and very handsome clerk in her father's firm are secured : a youth of eighteen, slim as a reed, and fair as an angel ; and Betha, seeing the scowl on Mr. Levison's face as he watches the rehearsals in the back drawing-room, thinks, half-fearfully, that Mattie's *fiancé* looks more like a murderer than a bridegroom.

CHAPTER XI.

ON the evening of the performance, the house
at Albert Gate is filled by a brilliant
assemblage of men and women; and amidst
the inspiriting strains of a brass band, the
lively hum of conversation, the sparkle of
jewels and the flash of eyes, few people have
leisure to observe the quiet girl dressed in
deep mourning who moves so unobtrusively
amongst the crowd, only anxious to escape
observation and to afford assistance wherever
it may be required. She takes no prominent
part in the display that follows, and yet it is
through her means alone that it proves to be
a complete success. She it is who arranges

a fold here or alters the position of a figure
there, who gives the signal for the curtain
to rise, and keeps her watchful eyes fixed
upon the silent actors the whole time it is
raised, that, at the first symptom of move-
ment on their part, she may order it to be
lowered again before they lose their self-
command.   The spectators exclaim, ' Beautiful !' ' Lifelike !' ' How admirably arranged !'
and loudly applaud the lay figures who present the living pictures ; but nobody dreams
that the brain that has conceived them, de-
signed them, and brought them to perfection,
belongs to the pale, handsome girl who keeps
in the background and shares in none of the
applause.   Nobody but Mr. Henderson, that
is to say, whose sharp, critical eyes watch all
Betha's movements with the greatest interest.   He is a stout, thickset man of middle
age.   His small features, which may once
have been handsome, are sunk between two
full cheeks, ruddy and polished as autumn
apples ; his grey hair is brushed all sorts of

ways, and his keen blue eyes seem to look
straight through you.   By nature Mr.
Henderson is kindly and tender-hearted, but
much hard rubbing with the world has given
him an upper crust of cynicism and suspicion
which is all the character he displays to
strangers.   He believes, like Carlyle, that
human nature is chiefly composed of fools—
and Mr. Henderson hates fools.

Because genius is so rare, he believes he
can detect it at a glance, and is ready to
worship it when once detected.

As the curtain falls upon the last tableau
and the strains of the band burst forth in a
seductive waltz, he moves to the side of Mr.
Kemyss.

' Who's that girl in black ?' he demands, in
his rough, curt way.

' What, the lady with the diamonds ?
That is Mrs. Benyon, the wife of the great
shipowner, Joseph Benyon of Liverpool.'

' No, no.   I don't mean her.   The girl in
a mourning dress who sticks so close to your
daughter ?'

'Oh, that is Miss Durant, an old school-fellow of Mattie's. Pretty little thing, isn't she?—but too quiet to suit my taste.'

'Don't know, I'm sure; haven't spoken to her yet. Looks to me as if there was a great deal in her.'

'Indeed! Now you mention it, I remember my daughter telling me she was thought very clever at the Princess College, for reciting and acting, and that sort of thing; but we couldn't persuade her to take any part in the performance to-night—she has so recently lost her mother—but she has been very active behind the scenes.'

'Humph! Just so!' says Mr. Henderson; and the upshot of the conversation is that he goes in search of Mattie, and a few minutes afterwards Betha is thrown into a fever of excitement by being asked to recite something for the benefit of the company. She is about strenuously to decline, but Mattie's persuasions overcome her scruples.

'*Do! do!* darling Betha! Papa wishes

it, and it will vex him so if you refuse, and
you can recite so beautifully, and they are all
dying to hear you, and you won't say *no* to
your own Mattie, will you, dear?'

Between the entreaty and persuasion of
her friend, and the fear of offending her host,
or appearing ungrateful for his hospitality,
Betha suffers herself to be dragged into the
midst of the company and announced as
about to give a recitation for their benefit.
She stands there for a moment, silent and
abashed, almost feeling as if no lines she has
ever learned will come to her assistance; but
raising her eyes to the assembly, she en-
counters the keen, critical glance of Mr.
Henderson fixed upon her, and the sight
seems to brace her nerves like steel. She
throws her head back proudly, her nostrils
dilate, her eyes glow, and she commences
those lines from the 'Idylls of the King'
which describe the last meeting between
Arthur and Guinevere.

The guests compose their persons and their

features decorously to listen. They are prepared to hear a schoolgirl's recitation of some
hackneyed speech from Shakespeare, or verses
of Cowper. Betha's opening description of
the King's arrival rivets their attention ; but
when her rich voice sinks to a monotone, and
she begins the lines :

> ' " Liest thou so low ! the child of one I honoured
> Happy, dead, before thy shame !' "

the listless men and the flirting women become
interested and serious, and more than one,
before the exquisite speech is concluded, has
a choking sensation in her throat, or smuggles
her pocket-handkerchief furtively to her eyes.
Betha neither sees nor hears the effect she is
producing. She is far away ; she has left the
drawing-room at Albert Gate and gone back
into the Past she tells of. She mourns with
Arthur—the sob that nearly chokes his
utterance has its ghostly copy in her own—
she looks through her unshed tears upon the
golden tresses with which Guinevere ' made

her face a darkness from the King,' and she
rides away with him in the mist, bereft and
alone ! As she comes back to herself and
receives the thanks of her audience, and
overhears their compliments upon her talent,
the bright lights dazzle her, she feels sick
and giddy—the grief of Arthur appears to
have renewed her own trouble, and she is
only anxious to get away to her room and be
quiet. It comes so natural to her to recite,
and to feel what she is reciting, she cannot
see anything wonderful in it ; these loud
plaudits and congratulations bewilder and
annoy her. Mattie does not oppose the fact
of her friend's retirement, because they are
going to dance, and she knows she would
rather not be present at that festivity. So
Betha is permitted to slip quietly away—
unnoticed, as she believes, by anybody, and
therefore she is the more surprised on reach-
ing the landing to find that she is followed
by the strange-looking gentleman whose
gaze she has encountered more than once

during the evening fixed earnestly upon her face.

'What is your name?' he demands abruptly, with his tablets in his hand.

Betha is considerably astonished at being asked such a question by a stranger, but as a friend of the Kemyss's she feels herself bound to be polite to him.

'Elizabeth Durant,' she answers.

'Ha! who taught you to recite?'

'Mr. Lillingstone, of Princess College.'

'Humph! you do him credit. Good-night;' and Mr. Henderson turns away with an uncouth nod.

She has hardly mounted six stairs, however, before he is after her again.

'Look here! Are you an orphan?'

Betha is about to say 'No,' when the remembrance flashes across her mind that no one could be more orphaned than herself, and she answers proudly:

'Yes, I *am* an orphan, and dependent on my own resources.'

'Humph! very good ; very good indeed,' replies the incomprehensible stranger, looking as pleased as if she had said she was heiress to ten thousand a year.

Betha would doubtless speculate very largely on this extraordinary behaviour on the part of Mr. Henderson, were it not put out of her head by finding a letter from Miss Denny on her dressing-table.

'She had written to that lady a few days before, telling her of the circumstances in which she was placed, and asking her advice as to her future movements. And Miss Denny writes back in the most elegant hand, on the most elegant paper, softly purring over the girl's misfortunes, covering up her aching heart, as it were, with a species of mental cold cream, and inviting her to a conference at the Princess College on the following morning, as she thinks it very probable she may be able to assist her.

'I know what that means,' thinks Betha bitterly to herself, as she throws the letter down upon the table; 'twenty pounds a year, and the drudgery of teaching the youngest class in the college. Oh, how little I thought, when I studied so hard to get the first place there, that it was to end in this!' and Betha does what she very seldom indulges herself by doing now: she breaks down utterly, and cries without restraint.

Yet she is too sensible to miss the opportunity that fortune may have in store for her, and the next morning, before Mattie's eyes are opened, she is seated in the private room of the Lady Superintendent of Princess College. But the conversation has not opened long before Betha finds that she has been summoned there not to be sympathised with, but quietly taken to task for her supposed rebellion against her father.

'The reason of my delay in answering your letter, my dear Elizabeth,' commences Miss Denny, primly, 'is because I could not possibly entertain any overtures on your part with regard to the college, nor give you a

personal recommendation elsewhere, until I
had ascertained what your good papa's views
were upon the subject.'

'My father's views!' cries Betha, aghast;
'but I told you plainly in my letter, Miss
Denny, that my father has turned me out of
doors because I refused to abandon my dying
mother. What on earth can have induced
you to appeal to him?'

'Ah, my dear, that is perhaps a young
person's view of the matter, but we sensible
elders see things in a different light. And
you were always impetuous and somewhat
headstrong, Elizabeth. It was your greatest
fault, you may remember, whilst under my
charge.'

'I have not been impetuous in this case,'
replies the girl, hotly. 'I went deliberately
to my father after three months' separation
and asked him to take me home again
(though I hated the very idea of going there),
and his answer was that I might beg in the
streets or starve before he would assist me.'

Miss Denny smiles incredulously.

'I think, my dear, there must be a little mistake somewhere, for Major Durant spoke very differently to me upon the subject. You were probably too much excited, Elizabeth, to know what was said or meant. Your papa seemed the perfect gentleman to me, and no gentleman could dream of turning anyone out of doors, far less a delicately 'nurtured young lady like yourself.'

'Ah! that is what the *world* thinks,' exclaims Betha, bitterly. 'Perhaps you imagine, Miss Denny, that no *gentleman* could insult his wife until his very servants cried shame upon him—that no *gentleman* could strike his children to gratify his malicious spite against their mother—that no *gentleman* could tell his daughter to her face that he hated her because her features did not resemble his own. And I agree with you— no *gentleman* would do this. But my father has done it, scores and scores of times, and

yet you think there must be "a little mistake somewhere!"'

And in repeating the words Betha un-
consciously imitates so closely the tone in
which they were uttered that Miss Denny
colours to hear the echo of her own voice.

'Dear, dear!' she is reduced to say con-
templatively, 'I really could not have believed all this unless you had told it me,
Elizabeth, with your own mouth. It is very,
very sad! Still, I should not have considered myself justified in proposing your
name as a teacher to the governors of the
college unless I had had your good papa's sanction to the proceeding. But I am happy to
say he gave it without hesitation, and seemed
to me only anxious to secure your welfare in
every possible way!'

'I refuse to come here on his sanction,'
says the girl, proudly. 'If you cannot give
me employment on my own merits, Miss
Denny, I will seek work elsewhere!'

'Now, my dear Elizabeth, pray do not be

so impetuous. Haste is always inelegant, and no lady who values the good opinion of society will ever permit herself to be betrayed into doing or saying anything that is not elegant. And this should be especially borne in mind by those who aspire to teach the young.'

'I shall never be "elegant," Miss Denny, in your sense of the word,' says Betha, curtly. 'Perhaps, after all, I was foolish to apply to you. I am fitter to serve in a shop or behind a bar than grind grammar and elegance into children!'

The lady superintendent closes her eyes with horror.

'My dear, *dear* Miss Durant! Pray think what you are saying, and never suggest anything so terrible in my hearing again. *Behind a bar!* If one of the governors were to hear that you even *knew* of such a calling I believe it would prevent your nomination. However, I am glad to be able to tell you that Major Durant having given his consent

to the proceeding, the governors offer you a
salary of fifteen pounds a year, as English
teacher, which is considered a very liberal
remuneration for the services of so young an
assistant.'

Betha is just about to declare that she will
not take the engagement, since they have
thought fit to apply for her father's authority, but her attention is diverted from that
circumstance by the clause that follows it.

' Fifteen pounds a year !' she exclaims.
' What am I to dress on, then ?'

Miss Denny looks mildly reproachful.

' The three youngest teachers in the
college receive the same salary, Miss
Durant,' she says, ' and I have heard no
complaints hitherto. I suppose you will
dress as those ladies do; and before midsummer arrives, let us hope that this unhappy difference with your papa will have
terminated, and that he will be enabled to
receive a good and dutiful daughter home
again for the vacation !'

'That he will *never* do!' replies Betha, determinately. 'Please understand it, once for all, Miss Denny! My father and I are separated for ever.'

'It is very, very sad!' reiterates Miss Denny, shaking her head. 'But what answer am I to convey to the college authorities, Elizabeth?'

Betha cannot make up her mind all at once. Fifteen pounds a year for nine months' ceaseless drudgery! She would rather, as far as her own feelings are concerned, be a charwoman on a couple of shillings a day!

'Give me a week to decide,' she answers; 'I am not prepared with an immediate reply. Tell the governors that I will write to them in a week.'

Miss Denny looks as if she thought Betha very ungrateful, and was sorry she had taken so much trouble on her account. She hardly embraces her at parting, but presents her cheek to be pecked at, and remarks coldly, that she trusts Miss Durant will keep to her

word, as the college authorities are not accustomed to be trifled with.

Betha returns to Albert Gate, slowly and
sadly, speculating on the probability of her
hearing of any other suitable work before
the week is ended. How little she thinks
that by that time the prospects of her
whole future will be entirely changed.

She enters the house languidly, but
brightens up on being told that Mr. Henderson is waiting to see her in the drawing-
room. Mr. Henderson, the mysterious
stranger who met and accosted her upon the
stairs last night. What on earth can he have to
say to her ? Curiosity wakes excitement in her
breast, and Betha runs upstairs, with a face
that a sudden glow has rendered beautiful.

CHAPTER XII.

'YOU WILL SUCCEED.'

MR. HENDERSON is standing in the orthodox British fashion, with his back to the fire, warming his coat-tails, and with a curious look of expectancy on his hard shrewd face. As Betha hastily opens the door, and comes towards him, her cheeks glowing with exercise and excitement, she looks so much handsomer than she did the evening before, that the old man regards her with the greatest satisfaction.

'What's your age?' he says, continuing his catechism as she advances to shake hands with him. Betha cannot help laughing. She has already guessed that her friend is an oddity and a genius, and she does not feel inclined to be offended at his curtness as she would at that of a younger man.

'Seventeen next month, Mr. Henderson.'

'I thought that was about it! And your height?'

'Five foot five.'

'Ah! and you'll grow another inch yet—a very good height too. Well, are you surprised to see me here to-day?'

'I don't know. I don't think I should be quite surprised at anything you did.'

'That's your opinion, is it? Well, I came to see you, and you only; so, as the servant told me Miss Kemyss was abed, and you awalking, I thought I'd wait till you returned. What mischief have you been up to, eh? Reciting in the park?'

'Oh dear no!' replies Betha; 'nothing half so agreeable! I've been over to the Princess College, by appointment, to receive the magnificent offer of fifteen pounds a year as a teacher. Isn't it noble? My aunt's housemaid used to have sixteen, and her beer-money into the bargain. I think I shall apply for her situation. It's the better of the two,' concludes Betha, sarcastically.

'And so you're really compelled to consider the advantage of receiving fifteen pounds a year, eh?'

'Yes! I told you yesterday that I am obliged to work for a living.'

'If I'm not much mistaken, I can put you in the way of work that will bring you in fifteen pounds a week instead,' says Mr. Henderson.

'*How?*' cries Betha, staring at him.

'We'll come to that by-and-by. I'll tell you first what brought me here this morning. I've got the management of some private theatricals to come off at the end of this week, in aid of some charity or other. Well, my principal lady's fallen sick, or got an attack of stage-fright, one of the two; and now, what do you say to taking her place for me?'

' *I*—to act on the stage, do you mean ? But how do you know I can *act*, Mr. Henderson ?' says Betha.

'How do I know you're a girl,' returns the visitor. 'Because I've got two eyes in my head, that's why! I heard you recite those lines of Tennyson's last night, and saw you act them too! That's enough for me! And now, will you take the part ?'

'Oh, thank you, Mr. Henderson! It is very kind of you to think of me; and I *love* acting so, I should enjoy it above all things!' exclaims Betha, her face beaming at the mere idea; 'only I am afraid I must say " *No !*" I am in such deep mourning, you see; and it would be contrary to all etiquette for me to appear in so public an entertainment as theatricals.'

'Humph! But you would go and teach brats, wouldn't you, in a public school ?'

'Yes ; but that I should consider my duty. It would be for money, too !'

' And so will this be for money. Look

here, child ; you've got the making of an
actress in you, and if you follow my advice,
you'll let me put you in the way of going on
the stage !'

'*Going on the stage !*' cries Betha, in a
tone very much like horror.

The notion has never suggested itself to
her in her life before. She has loved to see
plays and to study them ; has delighted in
her elocution lessons, and often won great
kūdos for her performances in amateur
theatricals : but that *she*, Elizabeth Durant,
should ever throw aside all the prejudices
of caste, and step upon the stage to sell her
talent for the benefit of the public, has never
entered her imagination. She knows that
many ladies are artists, and authors, and
poets : and that others sell their fancy-work,
and their voices, and their time : and she has
envied such women for their genius, and
admired their perseverance and ingenuity.

But to be *an actress !* To stand before
the footlights and deliver speeches and

imitate the gestures of humanity for common
men and women to laugh at or applaud, to
contemplate such a profession with pride, or
even with equanimity, Betha Durant has not
yet been long enough disentangled from the
conventional trammels that overhang the
lying face of modern society.

' Oh no !' she says, shrinking a little from
him, ' I *could* not ! You forget that I am a
lady !'

Mr. Henderson shrugs his shoulders and
gives a supercilious laugh.

' And you consider it more " ladylike," I
suppose, to teach brats their spelling? Why,
the one work is inspiration, and the other
drudgery ! However, take your choice, my
dear ; but I think I could have made something of you, all the same. And so you
won't help me out of my difficulty ?'

' Oh, I should like to do *that*, Mr. Henderson, if you think I could, and that people
would not consider it indecorous of me.'

' No one shall have the power to do so.

The other girl's name will remain in the bills, and you will only be taken for her. You'll make a first-rate Pauline—height, features, and everything—and I'll " coach " you up in the part.'

' Is the play " The Lady of Lyons " ? I know every word of it !' exclaims Betha.

' All the better. When can you come to a rehearsal ?—to-night ?'

' Oh, Mr. Henderson, it is very sudden ! What will Mattie say ?'

' I thought you told me you were your own mistress !'

' So I am ! But I refused to play in her tableaux last night !'

Mr. Henderson bursts into a hoarse laugh.

' And you think she may resent the omission ? First time I ever heard of one pretty girl being offended at the absence of another ! No, no, my dear ! Mattie Kemyss is a great deal too handsome not to forgive you for having refused to be a foil to her ! So, will you come ?'

' If Mr. Kemyss approves of it !'

' Kemyss has already given his consent, so that's settled. Now mind, half-past seven this evening, sharp, at St. Denis's Hall; and I'll be waiting for you at the box-office. Be punctual! Nothing is such bad form in our profession as coming to rehearsal imperfect, or behind your time !'

' *Our* profession, Mr. Henderson ! Are you then an actor ?'

' I *was*, my dear ! Now I am stage-manager of the Marlborough Theatre. Good-morning. I shall expect you sharp at seven-thirty !'

And in another minute Mr. Henderson has quitted the room, and Betha is left alone to try and realise the stupendous fact that she has consented to play Pauline in ' The Lady of Lyons,' at St. Denis's Hall, no later than the end of the week.

The events that follow her decision seem to justify Mr. Henderson's expectations. After four or five rehearsals, the important evening having arrived, Betha appears as

the Lady of Lyons at St. Denis's Hall,
looking very distinguished in the rich robes
which Miss Kemyss insists upon lending her,
and her personal attractions greatly enhanced
by the touch of rouge (which the exigencies
of the profession demand) upon her cheeks.
Her performance is naturally marked by
much crudeness and a touch of timidity, but
her Claude is a practised amateur, and
does nothing to hinder her efforts. Anyway,
she displays sufficient talent to call forth the
warmest admiration of her audience, and
decidedly carries off the honours of the
evening.

At the conclusion of the piece she is called
before the curtain and vociferously applauded,
and the papers that notice the performance
on the following day are unanimous in com-
mending her talent, and suggesting that if
she chooses to adopt the stage as a profession
there is a career before her. Betha hears,
and sees, and reads it all, and feels fairly
intoxicated with her success. The love of

histrionic display is inherent in her : it has lain dormant, hitherto, for want of encouragement ; but it is her second nature, and her present indulgence proves to be like the first drop of blood to the tiger.

Mr. Henderson's words and suggestions have recurred to her again and again during the rehearsals of the week. Indeed, the old gentleman has taken good care that she shall not forget them. And each time she thinks of the idea, it seems less and less offensive to her.

After all, there are good and well-born and virtuous women on the stage. Why should she not join their ranks, and use the talents God has given her to the best advantage ?

Mr. Henderson will not allow the favourable impression he has made to be effaced by time. The ' Lady of Lyons ' is played on the Saturday, and on the Monday he is at Albert Gate by eleven o'clock, just as Betha is considering, with horror, that she must refuse or accept Miss Denny's proposal by that night's post.

'You did very well, for a beginner,' says Mr. Henderson, alluding to the Saturday's performance; 'very well indeed, but no better than I expected of you. However, that was all play, and now we come to business. When are you going to take up this teaching that you talk of?'

'I—I—cannot tell,' stammers Betha. 'I must decide before to-morrow morning; but I hate the idea of being a governess so much that I hardly know what I shall say!'

'Naturally! It is throwing your talent into the gutter,' replies Mr. Henderson. 'And I could make a Mrs. Siddons of you in a few years. Think of that! A tip-top place in the profession! All the world at your feet, and fifty, perhaps a hundred, pounds a week, to lay by against the future. Isn't that better than teaching a lot of brats for fifteen pounds a year?'

'Oh, Mr. Henderson, of course it would be;

and, since my attempt last week, I have been thinking so much of what you told me. Only, I don't think you quite understand my position. I have no money, you know— none whatever; so, supposing I adopted the stage as a profession, how am I to live until I have secured a position by which I can maintain myself?'

Mr. Henderson looks at her admiringly.

' What a shrewd child it is ! Why, you've got the brains of seven-and-twenty, instead of seventeen. Now, look here! Can you speak the truth ?'

' Mr. Henderson ! what a question ! Do you suppose I ever speak anything else ?'

' Most of your sex do, my dear; so I thought you might be no exception to the rule. Did I understand you, then, to say that you are perfectly independent ?'

' I *am* independent. My mother is dead, and my father has repudiated me. I have no claim upon anybody.'

' And you would like to be an actress ?'

'I am sure I should *like* it !' replies Betha, discreetly.

'Very well. Then here's my proposition. I am a dramatic teacher, and I should like to bring you out as my pupil. I can't afford to keep you and teach you for nothing, because I'm not a rich man, and my time's my money ; but I've got a wife at home who'll be very pleased to take you in and look after you. And if you'll bind yourself down to me for an apprenticeship of three years, I'll provide for you during that time, give you lessons, and bring you out on the stage, taking, of course, your earnings as my pay ; and, after that time has expired, you'll be your own mistress and free to make your fortune. Is that a fair offer, or is it not ?'

'I don't know anything about the stage,' says Betha ; 'but it seems fair to me. Only, can I bind myself legally to you before I am of age ?'

'Don't know ; I'll find out. But, any way, I will take your written agreement.'

'Take care, Mr. Henderson. You may be trusting me too far,' says Betha, smiling.

'I don't think I can. You're a true girl, if ever I saw one. But I warn you it will be uphill work—at least at first.'

'I love work, and I am not afraid of it,' replies Betha. 'Only, if I should not succeed!'

'You *will* succeed. You may make up your mind to it. Do you suppose I should take all this trouble for love of you? No, no, my dear; you're a very nice girl, and a very pretty girl, but that sort of game wouldn't pay Mark Henderson. And now, if you've quite decided the matter, you'd better come round to my place this afternoon—there's the address—and see Mrs. Henderson, and arrange when you are to take up your abode with us.'

'What *will* Mattie say?' exclaims Betha.

'Possibly a good deal. Fools mostly do! But if you're the girl I take you for, you'll not be turned from your purpose by the opinions of anybody.'

Miss Kemyss *does* say a good deal, but it is not in the direction that Betha expected. She rather envies her friend going on the stage; she thinks it will be great fun, and wishes her papa were a poor man, that she might have an excuse for joining her. But she laments terribly over Betha's departure from Albert Gate. She almost thought she had secured her companionship for ever, and wishes a thousand times that that old wretch Henderson had never poked his stupid old head into their house on the fatal evening of the tableaux vivants.

'But I shall see you, darling Betha, shan't I—very, *very* often; and you will always call me your bosom friend and love me as you do now?'

'I shall always love you, dear Mattie; I can safely promise that, for no one could help doing so who knew how sweet and good you are. But as for seeing you, that must be as your father and Mr. Levison wish. I am perfectly aware that some people will consider

I have lost my social position in becoming an actress, and I shall respect their prejudices, whether I share them or not.'

' Betha, how can you say such a thing of papa, who is only too delighted if he can persuade actors and actresses to come to his house ; and as for Mr. Levison, I shall not choose my friends to please *him,* you may be well assured. I shall associate with whom I will, and, if he doesn't like it, he may do the other thing.'

' Well, dear Mattie, let us hope for the best l' replies Betha, with a sigh.

The path she has chosen does not appear all *couleur de rose* to her at that moment, poor child, whatever may lie in the future for her. She shrinks from the idea that her friends may think she has degraded herself, although her pride forbids her consulting any one of them in the matter.

' Aunt Janie is the only relative I possess to whom I owe anything,' she ponders ; ' and even she said she should be thankful to be quit of the care of me. Well, they *are* quit now, once for all. I shall never see any of them again, and the sooner they forget my existence the better !'

A few natural tears fall, as she remembers that little Hyacinth may grow up without even a sight of her face ; will forget perhaps that she ever had a sister Betha, or that the same mother loved and cared for them both. And mingled with that thought comes another, though a much less painful one—a passing wonder whether Mr. Frere, one of the few people who have spoken kindly to her of late, will be sorry to lose sight of her, or consider her beneath his notice if they meet. Yet, through it all, Betha feels in her inmost heart that she has chosen the lot for which she was intended, and that no private life, however happy, could raise in her breast the pleasurable emotions of hope and ambition that stir it every time she remembers that she is about to adopt the stage as a profession.

CHAPTER XIII.

'DON'T TELL MR. FRERE.'

ONLY one question puzzles her : shall she, or shall she not, inform her aunt Janie and Miss Denny of the occupation she has chosen to pursue? The idea of doing so is most distasteful to her; but Betha is both frank and brave, and argues with herself, that if she is not ashamed of becoming an actress, she should not be ashamed of owning it. Besides, sooner or later, all the world will hear of it, and she prefers to encounter any reproaches for her obstinacy, rather than to live in dread of being found out, and justly despised for her want of courage and deceit. So she sets off at once to Earl's Court,

which she reaches in the dusk of the April
evening. Mrs. Chapman and her daughter,
having just come in from a somewhat chilly
walk, are lounging over the fire and warming
their feet before going upstairs to take their
things off, when Betha is announced.

Aunt Janie receives the girl rather coolly.
She was very unwilling to maintain her
longer herself, but it is a rock of offence in
her eyes that anybody else should take the
liberty of doing so.

'Well, Betha! not tired of your fine
friends yet?' she says sarcastically, as her
niece embraces her.

'No, Aunt Janie, nor ever could be!
Nothing can exceed the kindness that has
been shown me at Albert Gate. I believe
Mr. Kemyss would let me live there for ever,
had I a mind to do so.'

'I should hardly think your pride would
permit you to do that. You used to talk a
great deal of your pride, Betha; but a
visit prolonged beyond the ordinary limits

becomes something very much like living on charity.'

'That is exactly my opinion, Aunt Janie ; and so you will be glad to hear that I am going to leave the Kemysses in a few days. I have got work to do, and I have pledged myself to do it for the next three years.'

Mrs. Chapman's listless face brightens. Here is really a bit of good news! Betha provided for, for the next three years, means at least Aunt Janie's immunity from marrying or maintaining her till the end of that period. For Mrs. Chapman has been much haunted the last few weeks by a nightmare vision of her niece returning, bag and baggage, on her hands.

'Have you really? Well, it will be the best thing for you. And what is the work, Betha? A companionship in India? I can't think of any other situation where they would tie you down to remain for three years.'

'No! it isn't India, nor anything half so

disagreeable as a companionship. I couldn't
undertake that sort of work, Aunt Janie; it
would drive me mad. I hope you won't be
vexed at what I have to tell you, but I have
made up my mind, and nothing will turn me
from it—I am going on the stage !'

'WHAT !' scream both Mrs. Chapman and
her daughter in one breath, and in the
biggest of capital letters.

'I intend to be an actress. I find I can
apprentice myself to a good master, who
will provide my maintenance, and teach me
my profession, until I can make an income
for myself; which in a few years I hope to be
able to do. And I like the stage ; and they
say I have talent, and am bound to succeed :
therefore I have decided to maintain myself
by that means, and no other.'

The girl brings out these words doggedly,
anticipating the storm of opposition they will
raise. By the time she has finished them,
Mrs. Chapman has recovered her breath.

'*An actress !*' she ejaculates; 'do you

know what you are talking about? With
what sort of people can the Kemysses have
allowed you to associate, to get such fearful
ideas into your head? Why, actresses are
the very scum of the earth—no respectable
people associate with them; and you will
be hated and despised by everybody you
have ever known.'

'They are *not* the scum of the earth,' replies Betha, firmly. 'There are just as good
women as yourself on the stage, Aunt Janie,
and most of them are talented far above the
ordinary run of people!'

'Talent! Rubbish! As if anybody could
not put on an immodest dress and kick about
her legs on the public stage. Its infamous—
horrible—fearful—I never heard of such a
thing in my life before, and you must be in-
sane to think of it.'

'Let them answer for it, then, who have
cast me forth to earn my own living,' replies
Betha.

'Oh! it's of no use accusing your poor

father of everything. I am sure he is the last person in the world to countenance such a disgraceful proceeding. And what's more, he shall stop it. For the credit of the family you must be prevented from committing such a moral suicide, and I shall go at once and tell Major Durant about it!' exclaims Mrs. Chapman, rising and re-assuming her gloves and furs.

'You may talk till you are hoarse, Aunt Janie,' replies her niece, as she also quits her chair; 'but you will not alter my determination. And my father has no power over me, thank Heaven! His day is over, and I am of an age to choose my own path in life.'

'Do you suppose, then, you are to be allowed to disgrace us all with impunity? What shall we be able to say when friends accuse us of being connected with *an actress?* And as to your cousin Blanche, you will never be allowed to speak to her again! I would not permit my girl to be contaminated by such association——'

'Perhaps I may learn to live even without that,' says Betha, 'and at all events, Aunt Janie, I could not live *on* it, without any more substantial nourishment. You seem to forget that I have to work for my *bread*, and must do it in the best way I can.'

'That is a mere excuse! I am sure Major Durant would allow you a sum for maintenance—indeed, he told me he had offered to do so——'

'And I would not accept it—nor ever will!' interrupts Betha. 'Let Major Durant keep his money for those who want it. I can maintain myself, and I will!'

Mrs. Chapman has no resource but to become pious.

'Oh, my poor, *poor* Mary!' she exclaims, with uplifted hands and eyes; 'it is well indeed that you were mercifully taken away from the evil to come.'

'Don't speak of my mother before me!' cries Betha, passionately; 'nor appeal to her to judge her child in the fashion that you do. Mother would have understood and sympathised with every feeling of independence I possess. *She* would not have left me to choose my own future without advice or guidance, and then have blamed me for doing the best I can for myself. There was no real likeness between my mother and you, Aunt Janie ; and if she sees us now, I know that she is on my side, and not on yours.'

'Oh, this is blasphemy !' exclaims Mrs. Chapman, preparing for flight ; 'but I shall go at once to your papa, and if he can be of any use in preventing you from carrying out your mad design, he will.'

'Good-bye, Blanche !' says Betha, holding out her hand to her cousin, as the door closes upon Mrs. Chapman.

'No, thank you, Elizabeth,' returns that young lady. 'If (as you say) you are resolved to disgrace us all, mamma will certainly not permit any acquaintanceship between us, and so the sooner it is dropped, I think, the better !'

'I quite agree with you,' says Betha, haughtily ; 'and I lowered myself by offering my hand to a woman who can forget she holds the position of a lady !'

And so the two cousins separate with angry feelings on either side. Meanwhile, Mrs. Chapman, having secured a cab, arrives at Northallerton Crescent, and invades the sanctity of Major Durant's home without ceremony. The major is annoyed at the intrusion, for, in the first place, he dislikes Mrs. Chapman for having befriended his wife and daughter ; and in the second, he is just about to set off to dine with the fascinating Mrs. Wallerton, and does not anticipate the prospect of delay. But his sister-in-law's business is soon disposed of.

'Major Durant, I have just received the most terrible piece of news. Elizabeth came to my house to announce that she has decided to go on the public stage for a livelihood !'

The major elevates his eyebrows.

'*Indeed !*'

' How can you receive it in such a fashion !
Are you not astonished—disgusted—angry ?
Fancy what a disgrace for the family ! What
will the world think of us ? Major Durant,
you must prevent it at all hazards.'

' Will you tell me how ?'

' Go to the girl—seek her out—place before her the enormity of the step she con-
templates taking in its proper light—say
you won't allow it—use your authority and
influence with her, Major Durant — for
Heaven's sake !'

' And of what avail will my authority be ?
Elizabeth is beyond it, and quite aware of
the fact.'

' And do you mean to say that you will
permit this outrage on society to be com-
mitted without an effort to prevent it ? You
ought to have the girl home. This is her
proper place, and you should *insist* upon her
returning to it !'

' I have already told you, Mrs. Chapman,

that I have no longer any right to insist. My daughter left my house and refused to be supported by me. I have nothing further, therefore, to do with her. She has severed the bond between us, and it must remain so !'

' And you will suffer her to go on the stage, then, to let all the world know that your daughter is a public actress ?'

The major winces slightly, but does not give in.

' She must go her own course, Mrs. Chapman ! It is nothing to me what she may do. And as to ever having her home again, that is entirely out of the question. My relations with Mrs. Wallerton are likely, before long, to assume a closer character, and Elizabeth has insulted that lady too grossly to allow of their ever living under the same roof.'

' Well, I call it disgraceful that you should allow your own child to go to rack and ruin in this heartless manner !' replies Aunt Janie with breathless indignation.

'Had you not encouraged my daughter in her first act of rebellion against me, Mrs. Chapman, perhaps this difficulty would not have arisen now. However, I have no more time at present to discuss the matter, and I hope you will do me the great favour of not referring to it in my presence again. My daughter Elizabeth is at all times a most unpleasant subject to me.'

'He has no more feeling than a log,' says Mrs. Chapman to Blanche, an hour later when detailing the circumstances of her visit to Northallerton Crescent, 'and I really begin to think that Betha takes after him instead of your poor dear Aunt Mary, for nothing could have been more heartless and ungrateful than her behaviour to me. And after my keeping her here for more than three months, fighting all her battles, and incurring so much expense on her account— to think of her going on the stage as a common actress! It is too—*too* much! I feel as if I should never get over it.'

' Well! the best thing we can do, in my opinion, mamma, is to ignore the whole business. Don't go telling everybody about it. Hardly any of our friends know Betha, and if they ask where she has gone, we can say abroad, or as a governess in the country, and drop the subject.'

' Yes ; that's an excellent idea, Blanche, and will at least save us the pain of confessing the dreadful disgrace she is to us. And above all things, my dear, don't tell Mr. Frere. He seemed very low and out of spirits the last time he called here, as if he were disappointed at not seeing Betha. I sincerely trust she has not gained any hold over the poor young fellow ; but a girl who can propose to be an actress must be bold enough for anything.'

' Oh, as to Bobby Frere,' replies Blanche, tossing her head, ' I don't suppose he is likely to care much about a pale dab of a girl like Betha ; but, nevertheless, I shall certainly not tell him where she has gone, because I know that actresses, and those sort of people, don't care what they do ; and perhaps she might make the poor boy marry her, or something dreadful of that sort, whether he wished it or no.'

'Yes ; it will certainly be wiser, for Mr. Frere's sake, as well as our own, that you should mention nothing before him of your unfortunate cousin's calling,' says Mrs. Chapman, discreetly ; and so, at last, they drop the subject.

Her interview with her blood relations does not leave Betha the better disposed to repeat the scene with the Lady Superintendent of Princess College, whose reproaches and cries of horror will be the harder to bear, because she has the less right to bestow them. So, by that evening's post she sends Miss Denny a letter instead, detailing the circumstances which have decided her to refuse the position of English teacher to the junior classes at fifteen pounds a year. Betha uses all her powers of composition to make the refusal a grateful one, and to disarm the probable prejudices of her late governess against the calling she proposes to adopt. The answer comes quicker than she anticipated.

On the afternoon of Tuesday, a perfumed, satin-laid envelope, addressed in the elegant caligraphy of the lady superintendent, is put into her hand. Betha opens it eagerly. Will Miss Denny be sympathetic, or tearfully reproachful ?

The folded sheet of paper inside falls out upon her lap. It is her own epistle returned to her, without comment or excuse.

CHAPTER XIV.

MR. AND MRS. HENDERSON are a strangely
assorted couple, living together in a noisy
street in the west central district of London,
as opposite as possible in their pursuits,
inclinations, and habits, and yet have passed
some forty years of wedded life with scarcely
a differing word. Mr. Henderson spends
most of his time out of doors or shut up in
his class-room. Mrs. Henderson hardly ever
leaves the house, and only knows the pupils
by sight. *His* life is passed amidst the active
turmoil of stage-management, the glare of
the theatre, and a medley of strange faces;
hers within the four walls of their private

house, minding her domestic affairs and looking after the cooking of her husband's dinner.
Mrs. Henderson never sees the inside of a
theatre ; the most successful piece that was
ever produced, or the greatest genius that
ever appeared, would not tempt her from her
fireside. ' Mr. Henderson does quite enough
of that sort of thing for both of us,' she is
wont to say. She is an old-fashioned homely
body, not unlady-like, though rather un-
polished, and the reception she gives to Betha
makes the girl feel at her ease at once.

'It will be quite a pleasure to me to have you
in the house, my dear ; though how you can
choose that nasty stage for a profession, I
cannot think. I'd rather do plain needlework
myself, than live in that heat and noise and
glare. However, there's no accounting for
tastes, as I tell Mr. Henderson, for I don't
believe he could exist without them. If you
were to set him down in the country, with
roses and lilacs to smell, and the fresh air to
blow in his face, I think he'd die. But

we've never had chick nor child of our own, you see, my dear, and so the theatre's a sort of a child to him; but it'll almost seem to me now as if I'd got a daughter in the house. And you'll take Trim out for a walk for me sometimes, I know; for I don't like to trust him to the servant, she's so dreadfully careless: and if I were to lose Trim, why, I should just go wild.'

Trim is a fat antiquated English terrier with whom Betha has already made acquaintance, and who appears to be as much of a stay-at-home as his mistress.

'Come now, old woman,' interposes Mr. Henderson, curtly; 'none of your nonsense! Miss Durant has come here to work and not to play, and she'll have other fish to fry than to turn whipper-in to that fat old mongrel of yours.'

Mr. Henderson speaks as sharply to his wife as he does to other people, but Mrs. Henderson does not appear to mind it. She

is used to his odd ways, and knows how kind
a heart lies beneath his rough exterior.

'Now, you know, we've got no time to
lose, and we must set to work at once,' he
says to Betha, the very first morning after
she has taken up her residence with them.
'No more Paulines nor Juliets nor
Lady Macbeths for you, my dear. You
must just put all such rubbish out of your
head, and attend to what I say to you.
You've talent, but you've everything to learn,
and we must begin at the beginning and work
our way up. For a month or six weeks I
shall give you daily lessons, and expect you
to practise hard by yourself in the interim.
At the end of that time (if you do your
duty), I may allow you to stand on the stage
for a few minutes occasionally in a crowd,
just to accustom you to the lights, but that's
all ; and you won't get that if you don't
please me ! Do you understand ?'

Betha is rather taken aback at first at the
idea of so slow a progress, but she is a

sensible girl, and resolves that it shall only incite her on to greater exertions. So she brings all her faculties to bear upon her master's instructions, and employs her spare time in exercising herself in gesture, and emphasis, and tone, until her brain becomes filled with one prevailing thought, and she cannot lie down to rest at night without dreaming of colloquial, rhetorical, and epic gestures; of rising, falling, and monotone inflexions : and natural, falsetto, and orotund voices.

Mr. Henderson is delighted with her progress, and, even before the month has expired, she is allowed the supreme privilege of accompanying him to the Marlborough Theatre every night, and standing on the stage as one of a crowd of evening visitors, in the last act of a new comedy. But before that moment arrives, there is a discussion as to what name she shall assume for her professional career. Mr. Henderson is very contemptuous on the subject of changing her

name, for he considers the histrionic so grand
an art that no name can be too good for its
professors. And so might Betha think,
except for her family. They have not been
very considerate of her feelings, but she has
no wish to outrage theirs, more than is absolutely necessary. Therefore it is decided
that she shall adopt her second name of
Selwyn (which was also her mother's maiden
name), and as Elizabeth Selwyn she is introduced behind the scenes of the Marlborough
Theatre. She has to change her dress on
arriving there, and for that purpose is con-
ducted to the dressing-room of the second
ladies. Betha stares aghast at the apartmemt
she is directed to enter. She knew that
everything behind the scenes of a theatre is
very different from what it is in front, but she
was not quite prepared for the squalid and
dirty appearance of the second ladies' dressing-room. White-washed walls; an uncar-
peted floor, black with the marks of boots
that have tramped through the mud to the

theatre ; half-a-dozen gas-lights flaring and unprotected ; three half-crown mirrors (one without a frame), set up upon a deal shelf against the wall, which also bears a couple of cracked and filthy basins and a jug without a handle, half filled with cold water—such is its aspect. Betha has never been in so rough and dirty-looking a place before, and she stands upon the threshold, with her bundle in her hand, gazing timidly at four or five girls in various stages of undress, who are preparing themselves to obey the summons of the call-boy.

' Hullo ! who's that ?' cries one of them sharply, as the opening of the door attracts her attention. ' Come in, do ! and don't stand there, letting that abominable draught blow on my shoulders. What's your business ?' she continues as Betha closes the door and enters the room ; ' brought a dress for anybody ?'

' No, this is my own dress.   I am one of Mr. Henderson's pupils. He wishes me to go on in the last scene this evening.'

'Oh, one of old Henderson's pets, are you? Then I suppose we shall all be expected to do the "kow-too" business to you ; but you won't find *me* do it, for one. What's your name ?'

' Elizabeth Du—I mean Elizabeth Selwyn.'

' Well, mine's Riley. Come on, Selwyn, since you are here, and help me to lace up this bothersome dress. I'm on in the second act, and you're not wanted till the third, so you've lots of time.'

' I shall be happy to assist you, Miss Riley, if I can,' replies Betha, courteously. The girl bursts into a coarse laugh.

'Just listen to her, Tomkins. *Miss Riley!* Couldn't you tell she was a greenhorn at a glance ? How rum these beginners are ! They always kill me with laughing.'

' Are you never polite to one another, then, at this theatre ?' demands Betha gravely, as she laces the young lady's dress. Her companions shock her far more than the appearance of the dressing-room.

'Oh no, my dear! 'tisn't that. We're
ready enough to help each other. It's all
" give and take " with us here, as you'll soon
find out; but we've no time to be " missing "
and " madaming " one another. But hullo!
there goes the curtain. Give me the rouge,
Wilson, there's a dear! If I'm late again to-
night, I shall get a confounded wigging from
old Henderson.'

And, as the call-boy's voice is heard outside the door, Miss Riley runs off, and is lost
to view.

Betha undoes her parcel, and silently prepares to change her dress. The other girls
are chattering volubly of their admirers, and
their dresses, and their parts ; whilst her
proud nature is writhing under the familiarity
with which she has been treated, although
she knows that if she is wise she will trample
all such feelings under foot. Yet, at first, to
a delicately nurtured girl, brought up carefully amidst gentlemen and gentlewomen, it
is hard to bear. Having unpacked her

parcel, she advances to one of the basins to wash her hands.

' You drop that soap—it's mine,' cries Miss Tomkins, as Betha touches the piece of yellow soap that lies beside the basin.

' Lor, Tomkins! how sharp you are!' says another of the girls; 'how was she to know that, and on the first day, too? Here, my dear!' she continues, with good-natured familiarity to Betha, 'you take my bit. We're all obliged to provide our own soap here, but you'll know better another time, won't you, and bring some for yourself.'

' Oh yes! thank you,' replies Betha, with something very like a sob in her throat. ' Mr. Henderson ought to have told me. Of course, I am quite ignorant of the rules of a theatre!'

' And you've never been on the stage before to-night?'

' Not on a public stage!'

' And you're a lady, aren't you?'

' Yes!' says Betha, proudly. ' I *am* a

lady ! but I am apprenticed to Mr. Henderson for the next three years, and therefore I
am bound to do just what he tells me.'

'Prenticed to Henderson, are you ? Well,
you're safe enough then, my dear ; for he's a
power here, and no mistake, and we shall all
have to mind our P's and Q's with you.'

And Betha finds these words to be correct,
for both Miss Riley and Miss Tomkins
greatly abate the roughness of their speech
when they find out who she is, though to
bear their sarcasm quietly when they address
her as 'my lady !' and ' Henderson's pet,' is
almost more difficult to her. She tells Mr.
Henderson frankly of her disappointment,
and he laughs at it.

'You must begin at the beginning,' he
says ; ' and if you don't rough it a bit at first,
how will you appreciate the difference when
you get on in the profession ? I know
Tomkins and Riley are a little wild—they all
are—but you must forget you're anything
but a woman, and try and sympathise with

them. They've not had your advantages, remember; and if they talk roughly, they've warm hearts at the bottom, like most of the sex, and will show them fast enough if you'll let them.'

And Betha, acting on this advice, soon makes friends with the second ladies, and finds that a kind word here and a little assistance there causes them speedily to agree that ' Selwyn isn't half-bad,' and wins their goodwill in return.

It is a gala night with Betha when she has her first lines to speak in public. It has seemed so hard to her, who has whole plays in German, and French, and English by heart, to stand at the back of the stage and say nothing. The first effort Mr. Henderson allows her to make is a very simple one. She has only to play the part of a waiting-maid in some farce, but she does it so brightly and ingenuously—her eyes say so much when she is not speaking—and her features and intonation are so good, that the principal actor

is delighted with her, and her master gives
her warm praise.

'Getting on!' he says that night, at supper,
rubbing his hands. 'Getting on! I shall
live to see the girl play Siddons' parts yet,
old woman; but she must creep before she
crawls.'

'La, Mark! I wish you wouldn't talk
about creeping and crawling. It always
makes me remember the black-beetles; and if
Trim touches my foot with so much as the
tip of his tail, under the table, I'm safe to
scream.'

And so Betha works her way steadily
onwards; learning any number of parts for
future use, and never shirking trouble in
order to perfect, as far as lies in her power,
the instructions she receives from her master.
And Mr. Henderson is faithful to his trust.
He would have proved so, perhaps, under any
circumstances; but he has his own interests
to work for here, and nothing sharpens a
man's energy so much as having a pecuniary

benefit contingent on his labour. He goes through all the best-known female parts with his pupil ; and though he will not permit her to speak more than a dozen lines upon the stage, she has the characters of Rosalind, Beatrice, Juliet, Pauline, Constance, and half the heroines of old and new comedy and tragedy, at her fingers' ends.

Meanwhile, though she is so engrossed by her work that it leaves her little leisure for sad thoughts, it must not be supposed that Betha has entirely forgotten her old friends in the old world she appears to have left behind her. Mattie Kemyss—who is to be transformed into Mattie Levison before many months are over—she often sees, and of her sister Hyacinth she is constantly dreaming vague and painful dreams. The summer is now at its height, and the London season nearly finished.

Mrs. Henderson insists upon Betha taking a walk every day; and accompanied by Trim, wheezing audibly at the unwonted exertion, she often finds her way up to the Regent's Park, and loiters about the precincts of Northallerton Crescent, in hopes of meeting her little sister and Bentham. But her efforts seem all in vain. Never once has she caught a sight of either her father or Hyacinth, until she begins to think they must have left the district and gone to live somewhere else.

One afternoon, however, as she is calling and whistling to old Trim, who is deaf as well as wheezy, to come out of the road before he is run over by the omnibus, her voice attracts the attention of a smartly-dressed young lady who is walking some distance in front of her, accompanied by a servant, and whose face Betha immediately recognises as that of her sister. She cannot doubt her eyes, but she would never have known the child had she not turned round.

Betha is still clad in the mourning crape, now somewhat rusty and dusty, which she put on eight months before, in memory of her mother : but Hyacinth is dressed in a smart costume of blue and white, and wears two blue feathers in her hat, with a bunch of pink rosebuds. Her dark hair is plaited in a long tail behind, tied with blue ribbon, and she looks as festive and fashionable as it is possible for so young a lady to appear. Still it is Hyacinth—her own little sister and her mother's darling—and Betha springs after her with a cry of delight.

'Cinthy, Cinthy! didn't you know me? I have been walking up and down here for days in hopes of seeing you. I am so glad that we have met !'

Hyacinth looks at her sister inquiringly for a moment, and then draws herself back primly.

'I mustn't speak to you, Elizabeth! I told you so before ! Papa has particularly forbidden me to say a word to you !'

The tears start to Betha's bright eyes at the coolness of her address.

'Oh, he could not be so cruel, darling !

You are my own little sister, you know, and I cannot harm you by a few words——'

'Who is this young lady, Miss Durant?' demands the maid in charge of the child.

'It is my sister, THE ACTRESS, Mary,' replies Cinthy in a low voice, but not so low but that Betha hears the emphasised words; 'and you know that papa particularly forbid you to stop if we met her.'

'Well, then, miss, you'd better come home at once, or I shall get in a scrape, maybe, with Mrs. Durant!'

'With *whom*?' exclaims Betha, hurriedly.

'With mamma,' replies Hyacinth. 'Don't you know that we have a new mamma—at least *I* have, for she wouldn't be *your* mamma. She says you have disgraced yourself, and you dance and sing and get money, and no one will ever speak to you again.'

'It is untrue—it is untrue,' murmurs poor Betha; 'and it is wicked and cruel of them to tell you so, Cinthy. I shall never do any-

thing to disgrace you, nor our dear mother in
heaven ; and I would never call any other
woman " mamma," and so it matters nothing
to me whether she wishes to be my mamma
or not.'

' Miss Durant, you'd better come home,'
says the servant, warningly.

' So I will when I've told her something,'
replies Hyacinth. ' But you *do* dance and
sing, don't you, Betha ? Mamma—that is
Mrs. Wallerton, you know, only now she's
called Mrs. Durant—isn't that funny ? and
we don't live in Northallerton Crescent at
all, but a much bigger house—she won't let
me speak of you. She says that I must
forget *my sister, the actress*, as soon as ever
I can, or else everybody will despise and
spit on me !'

' Oh, Hyacinth ! this is the hardest part
of it all !' cries Betha, sobbing ; ' and what
can I say to make such a child as you understand ? Only ask Bentham ! Dear old
Benty will do me justice, and tell you that

sister Betha will never do anything that is disgraceful or wrong.'

'Benty can't tell me,' says Cinthy, 'because she's gone away. She's been gone ever so long. And Mary's my maid now—my maid and mamma's—and I go to school in the mornings, and some day mamma will take me to a circus, but not to a theatre, for fear I might see you there.'

'And didn't you *want* to see me, Hyacinth?' says Betha, reproachfully.

'Yes, a little; but mamma says I'm Miss Durant now, and the only daughter; if you came back I shouldn't be! And I'm to have all mamma's rings and her watch and chain—the dead mamma's, you know—and when I'm grown up I shall wear them!'

'Good-bye,' says Betha, mournfully; 'I see they have set you against me, Cinthy, but you were mother's darling all the same, so God bless you, my dear, dear little sister, and may you always have some one to love you as well as your poor Betha does.'

And Betha runs off, unable longer to keep
back her streaming tears and choking sobs,
until she is stopped by the alarming, apo-
plectic attempts of Trim to keep up with her,
and stifles her own feelings in order to save
the poor old animal. Her father re-married
after eight months of widowhood, and Hyacinth taught to regard her name as a burning
disgrace. Truly her home (could she re-
enter it) would no longer be home to her.
She cries herself nearly blind over the encounter of the afternoon, and is quite relieved
by a piece of intelligence which Mr. Henderson delivers to her at the supper-table, and
which at any other time would have filled
her with dismay at the prospect of a fresh
separation and a new home.

'I've got a letter here from my friend
Cheyne,' he says—'a fine fellow, Cheyne,
proprietor of the Buton and Byton Theatres,
and one of the kindest-hearted men in England. Half of our best actors and actresses
have matriculated at Buton ; I call it the

nursery of English dramatic art. Well, my
dear, I've been writing to Cheyne about you,
and he's willing, on my recommendation, to
give you an appearance on his boards. I am
afraid you won't be quite so cosy as we've
been here. There ain't an old woman like
mine at every corner, you know ; but Cheyne
has a niece at his theatre whose rooms you
can share, and I dare say you'll come to some
arrangement with her about your board.
Anyway, Cheyne will pay you a pound a
week till you're worth more to him, and you
must do the best you can on that.'

'Oh, I am sure it will be ample,' says
Betha, who has no idea of the expense of
housekeeping, 'but I thought *you* were to
take my salary, Mr. Henderson. Won't
Mr. Cheyne pay you something too ?'

'That's between him and me,' replies the
manager, with his mouth full ; 'anyway, you
be a good girl, and live quietly and respect-
ably on your share, and as soon as Cheyne
raises *me* I'll raise *you*. You'll have capital

practice down at Buton, and first-rate management. Work well, and do as you're told,
and you shall come back to London before a
twelvemonth's over your head.'

' Oh, how good you are to me !' cries
Betha, gratefully ; 'indeed I will work as
hard as ever I can, if it were only to see you
and dear Mrs. Henderson again !'

Mrs. Henderson weeps copiously at parting
with her adopted daughter, and abuses those
' nasty theatres ' for a couple of days before
she quits them, when she actually ventures
out of doors, for about the first time in a
twelvemonth, to accompany Betha to the
railway station, and leave her in a third-
class carriage, with a packet of sandwiches in
her hand, all properly booked and labelled
for Buton.

CHAPTER XV.

'BE A GOOD GIRL.'

MISS KATE MONTALAMBERT, with whom
Betha is to share her rooms at Buton, is a
specimen of the old actress who can never
forget that she has been young. She is
waiting at the railway station, by her uncle's
request, to receive the new recruit, and comes
tripping along the platform as she catches
sight of Betha with a juvenile spring that
might have belonged to a girl of twenty.
She is attired in a very juvenile fashion also;
her face is tightly covered with a spotted
veil, and is almost as much 'made up' as it
is by night.

'This is Miss Selwyn, I presume,' she

says jauntily. 'Well, my dear, uncle asked me to come and meet you, as he thought you would feel strange at first; and so we'd better drive straight home, and have our dinner before we go down to the theatre.'

'But I haven't anything to do to-night, surely?' says Betha, alarmed at the idea that she may be expected to appear in a new part at an hour's notice.

'You're not *on* yet, but of course you'll put in an appearance. Why, I go down every night of my life, whether I play or not. I couldn't spend an evening at home if you were to pay me for it.'

'I suppose you'd miss the music and the company?' says Betha, laughing.

'My dear, I'd miss everything. The gas, and the chatter, and the orchestra, and the calls—well, there, you might as well put me in a prison at once, as ask me to sit at home of an evening and mope. If I have only a pair of stockings to darn, I stand at the

wings and darn 'em there. I don't believe I
could anywhere else.'

'I suppose you've been a long time on the
stage, then, Miss Montalambert ?'

'All my life, child. I used to go on as a
fairy in uncle's pantomimes at three years
old—Buton is celebrated for its Christmas
Pantomimes, as I dare say you've heard—
and I stayed with him till sixteen ; and then
I went out on my own hook, worse luck !—I
wish I'd never done so—but uncle couldn't
do without me, you see, so here I am again,
and as likely to die at Buton as not.'

By this time they have reached Miss
Montalambert's lodgings, which are small
but comfortable, although the forks laid on
the little round table for dinner are of steel,
and the cruet-stand of a doubtful metal that
looks as if it had been dug up from
Pompeii.

'Baked shoulder of mutton and onion
sauce, my dear. Hope you like it,' cries
Miss Kate gaily, as she casts aside her hat

and veil and displays a middle-aged, thin, and
puckered face, the lines in which pearl
powder and glycerine are powerless to con-
ceal. 'I have a capital plan here. I pay
the woman of the house ten shillings a week
for my board, without liquor, you know, and
dine from the family joint. She'll do the
same by you, and you'll find it a great saving.
Then, the rooms are ten shillings a week also,
everything included ; so if you don't mind
sharing my bed, fifteen will see you clear.'

'It isn't a question of *minding*,' replies
Betha, ingenuously ; 'I must do it whether
I like it or not, because I'm only to have a
pound a week for the commencement.'

'Bless you, child! I began on ten shillings,
and managed to live on it, too. But how
"green" you are ! Here's nature, and no
mistake,' says Miss Montalambert, playfully
pinching Betha's cheek ; 'but don't go and
tell everybody what you get. They'll think
all the more of you if they believe your
salary to be double.'

'Will they?' demands Betha with open eyes; 'but I want them to like me for what I can do, not for what I can *earn*. Though I suppose they will think the one depends on the other.'

'No, they won't, my dear. Most of them won't think at all. They haven't the brains to do it. But if you're a hard worker you'll get on with uncle. He's always scolding me for being such an idle thing, and liking play too well.'

And Miss Kate looks so wicked that Betha begins to question if she has made a mistake, and her companion is four-and-twenty instead of four-and-forty, despite her general appearance.

'It will be such a comfort to have your protection to and from the theatre,' Miss Montalambert begins again presently, as she glances at the golden-haired girl, young enough to be her daughter, who is devouring all she says. 'You can't think how awkward it has been for me living alone. There are so many idle young fellows in Buton—as in all large towns—and they do *persecute* one so.'

' In what way ?' asks Betha.

'Why, by following you, my dear ; and writing you letters, and sending you flowers, and all that sort of nonsense.'

' People whom you do not know ?'

'Yes ; gentlemen who have seen me at the theatre, and been foolish enough to lose their hearts to me. It's really dreadful ! I tell uncle sometimes he'll have to provide me with an escort, and he says the best thing I can do to protect myself is to marry again !'

' Have you been married, then ?' says Betha.

' Oh yes ! foolish thing that I was ! I was married when a mere child. My mother ought to have whipped me and sent me to bed instead ; however, I would have my way, and spoil all my chances. My real name is Potter—Mrs. Henry Potter—but

I've been a widow for several years, and
these silly fellows know I'm free again, and
want to persuade me to make a fool of
myself for the second time. But no, no!
they can't catch Kate Montalambert sleeping,
my dear! I like my liberty too well, and
mean to enjoy it. It will be time enough
to think of marrying again when I am an
old woman.'

Betha thinks that if Miss Kate—or Mrs.
Potter—(she hardly knows which to call her)
intends to wait much longer, she will be too
old to marry at all; but naturally she does
not say so.

'Have you any children?' she demands,
after a pause.

'Yes, one! my little boy. Mamma's pet,
as you may imagine. But I never take
the child about with me. It would not be
good for him; and I should be in constant
anxiety on his account whilst I am at the
theatre.'

And indeed, as 'mamma's spoilt pet' is

(as Betha subsequently ascertains) nearly
eighteen years old, and earning his own
livelihood in an iron foundry, it would be
both inconvenient and embarrassing for Miss
Kate Montalambert to encounter any of the
youthful adorers of Buton with a son by her
side of nearly their own age.   But this new
phase of human weakness amuses Betha
more than it repulses her, for Mrs. Potter
believes so firmly in her own attractions that
she has no idea that the rest of the world is
laughing at her.

She has been so long on the boards of her
uncle's theatre, that she quite thinks she possesses some authority there, and (Mr. Cheyne
being a widower) might make strangers at
first believe the same.   But though she
paces the green-room each night, and stands
about at the wings as though the whole
place belonged to her, ordering the carpenters
and scene-shifters about, and directing the
actors as to their parts and portions, no one
ever takes the slightest heed of her com-

mands ; and '*Only old Kate at her larks !*'
is a by-word in the Buton Theatre Royal.

Betha is very much pleased on entering
the theatre that evening, to find that Mr.
Cheyne is about to entrust her with a *real
part*—indeed with seven or eight real parts!
—all of which he crams into her hands in
the course of their interview, telling her to
study them at once, so as to be able during
the ensuing week to fill the place of a young
lady under notice of dismissal.

Had he crammed Betha's hands with bank-
notes instead, he could not have delighted
her more.   She receives his orders with
glowing cheeks and kindling eyes ; and Mr.
Cheyne thinks, as he regards her, ' That if
Henderson is not mistaken in her talent, the
shrewd old manager knew what he was about
when he picked up that girl for the stage and
apprenticed her to himself.'

' But look here, my dear,' he says, as their
first interview is brought to a conclusion,
' let me give you a caution.   You are going

to live, I believe, with my niece, Kate Montalambert. Well, Kate's a good girl— a very good girl indeed!'—(Mrs. Potter speaks of herself so continually as a girl that her friends are beginning to think she must be one)—'but she has no brains, and she's a deal too fond of flirting and flattering. Now don't you let her fill your head with a lot of nonsense about young men, and bouquets, and diamond rings. It's all lies, my dear!—all lies! I've been a manager for forty years, and I never knew any young woman come to good who believed in such rubbish. The good girls *may* get diamond rings in the *next* world—I know nothing about that—but I'm quite sure they don't get 'em in this. And as I feel in a measure responsible to my friend Henderson for your behaviour, I hope you'll remember what I say. Stick to your work, and make up your mind to do without lovers for the next ten years, or you'll end where poor Kate is—at the beginning!'

By which advice it may be presumed that
' uncle' has not so high an idea of his niece's
genius and personal attractions as Mrs. Potter
herself would lead you to believe.

CHAPTER XVI.

'I CANNOT STAY AT BLACK ABBOTTS.'

BETHA attends faithfully to Mr. Cheyne's instructions, and discourages, as much as possible, Mrs. Potter's revelations concerning her mysterious admirers; the secret assignations they implore her to make; the frantic letters they write, and the valuable presents she is forced to return to them. And indeed it is no sacrifice to the girl to forego such conversation. She has a refined and modest nature. Anything that savours of coarseness—especially with regard to love or marriage—shocks and distresses her, and Miss Montalambert's careless manner of speaking of the young chemists, grocers,

and wine merchants who follow in her train,
is especially offensive to Betha, who often
wishes that ' the glorious army of martyrs,'
as Miss Kate facetiously designates them,
were really dead of the love they are supposed to be dying for.   But Betha busies
herself with her play-books and with altering
her wardrobe to meet the coming emergen-
cies, and so avoids the dreaded topic as much
as possible.   In this employment she finds
Miss Montalambert's aid invaluable.   No
one can twist and turn a dress so as to suit
half a dozen parts like the kittenish actress,
nor make five shillings spread itself out in
laces and ribbons to furbish up as many old
robes to look like new.   And though Mrs.
Potter's brain is weak and her vanity inordi-
nate, her heart is in the right place ; and
Betha, lonely and friendless in the world, can
forgive her every foible, for the sake of the
affection she lavishes upon her.

No jealousy exists between them, even
when, after a few weeks' practice, the young

girl is elevated to a post which is far above that held by her companion. Miss Kate's faith in herself is so complete, that it leaves no margin even for envy of others. If she is allotted the worst part, she only thinks that ' uncle ' has done it to spare her.

' He knows I work so hard in the theatre, dear,' she confides to Betha, ' looking after the men and the scenery, and the wardrobe, that he is afraid I shall break down if he imposes too great a mental strain upon me. Dear, dear ! whatever will he do if one of these foolish fellows over-persuades me to become a bride again ! I couldn't look after both their interests at once, could I, Betha ? and I really think it would break the old man's heart to lose me !'

So Miss Montalambert's stream of life glides calmly on, without a ripple to disturb its equanimity. There are no people so happy in this world as those who are perfectly contented with themselves. Betha does not feel so. She makes a very credit-

able *débût* at the Buton Theatre, and Mr.
Cheyne gives her plenty of study and plenty
of practice.

Country theatres cannot afford to let their
pieces have a 'long run,' as they do in
London. Their patrons demand variety
above all other things, and a constant
change is absolutely necessary; sometimes
two or three times a week.

Mr. Cheyne seems determined to put
Betha through her paces, 'and see of what
metal the girl is made,' so that during the
course of a few months she maintains no
less than thirty or forty different characters.
On Monday she will personate a chamber-
maid, on Wednesday an old woman, and on
Saturday perhaps a duchess. Sometimes
she has, with many a blush, to don garments
that are distasteful to her feelings; but
Mr. Cheyne pooh-poohs all objections, and
maintains that she must try every style of
art, until she has settled down into her proper
position.

Still, although this is the life she has
wished for and chosen for herself, Betha is
not quite happy nor contented. Something
seems out of gear with her or her performance. She goes on plodding through the
parts allotted her — sometimes with more
zest and pleasure than at others — but yet
not with her heart quite in her work, and
almost tempted on occasions to doubt if her
friends have not made a mistake in thinking
that she possesses more than ordinary ability
for the stage. But Mr. Cheyne seems satisfied with her efforts, and Mr. Henderson writes
her encouraging letters, and so the girl tries
to believe the fault must lie with herself, and
that the cold and the damp of the autumn
have had some lowering effect upon her
energies.

Christmas arrives, and with it the inevitable pantomime, in which there is no part
for Betha. Miss Kate Montalambert, who
has arms like lucifer-matches, and legs like
drumsticks, and the remains of a very squeaky

soprano voice, has played the Queen of the
Fairies in her uncle's pantomimes ever since
she was three years old (as she takes good
care to inform the public), and refuses to give
up the part. So that arrayed in a very few
yards of white satin, and a great many
ounces of spangles, Miss Kates drives her
' army of martys ' to distraction every night,
precisely at eight o'clock, whilst her young
companion sits at home, thankful for the
solitude and rest, poring over Shakespeare,
and Sheridan Knowles, and Lytton, and
dreaming of the days when she may have
a chance of putting her studies to some
advantage.

' Is it not provoking, Betha ?' smirks Mrs.
Potter one morning over the breakfast-table ;
' that tiresome creature, Ashton, would insist
upon stealing one of the bouquets from my
dress last night, and declared he should keep
it till he died. As if the silly thing would,
you know ! But I must have some more
flowers for to-night—it's that artificial haw-

thorn that we bought at Harrison's, over the bridge—and I'm so tired I feel as if I could hardly drag one leg after the other.'

'I'll go for you,' exclaims Betha. 'I know the shop well, and the hawthorn too. There was a lot of it in the window yesterday.'

'Oh, you dear, good-natured darling!' cries Miss Kate, enthusiastically. 'Well, if you don't mind, *do* get me half-a-dozen sprays' (they were twopence halfpenny each, I think), 'for young Mr. Cook very nearly carried off a bunch as well, and I dare say I shall have a repetition of the scene to-night. It really is very provoking!'

'If you continue to supply all your admirers at this rate I'm afraid you'll soon be ruined, Kate,' says Betha, with a smile.

'Oh, my dear! what *can* I do? They insist upon it, you know. I really almost wish I had not taken the part of Fairy Queen this season. The dress is so conspicuous, and makes one look so absurdly young. Mr. Ashton told me last night he had a bet on with another gentleman as to whether I was twenty-two or twenty-six !'

There is little doubt as to Betha's age as she sallies forth to do her friend's commission. Her soft golden hair, her pure complexion, her dewy grey eyes, the bloom upon her cheek, all betoken the glow and elasticity of sweet seventeen. She goes bounding along the frosty pavement, wishing she were not too old and dignified to run a race with the dirty urchins that are scampering over the road, and inhaling fresh draughts of life with every healthy, full-drawn respiration. She still wears her mourning robes, but they are relieved now by bunches of violets that nestle most becomingly against her golden hair and alabaster skin.

She enters the linen-draper's shop quickly, and with a little clatter that attracts the attention of two young ladies at the counter, and in another moment Betha is astonished to hear her own name loudly ejaculated.

' Betha—Betha Durant !' exclaims a voice

which seems familiar to her; 'where on earth
do you spring from?' and before she has
time to answer the question four arms are
cast about her neck and a vehement shower
of school-girl kisses descends on her unprotected cheeks.

She looks up in amazement to recognise
two of her companions at Princess College
— Ada and Ella Matthews, the sisters
of happy memory in connection with that
memorable duet on two pianos, in which the
one came up to the winning-post a full length
behind the other.

'And who would have thought to see
you?' replies Betha. 'This *is* a surprise,
Ada. Why, it is a year since we parted!
And how you and Ella have grown! You
must be half a head taller than I am.'

'Oh yes! mamma calls us monsters, but
we left the college at Midsummer, Betha;
and papa's place, Black Abbotts, is only about
eight miles from Buton.'

'How I wish you would come out and

stay with us there! Do, do come, Betha! come back with us now. That is our phaeton at the door, and we shall just be in time for luncheon if you'll make haste.'

'My dear Ada, what an idea! As if I could possibly go to Black Abbotts without an invitation from your mamma,' says Betha. 'Besides,' she adds, a little more timidly : 'I don't think I *could* stay with you now, under any circumstances.'

'Oh, mamma shall ask you fast enough. I'll make her write the invitation as soon as ever we get home. She is always so pleased for us to see our friends, because it's awfully dull out there after London, and there's heaps and heaps of room, isn't there, Ella ?'

'But perhaps Betha's friends won't like her to come,' suggests Ella. 'Are you staying in Buton, Betha ?'

'No ; I am living there,' she answers, with a blush, anticipating the queries that will follow.

'Living in this horrid, dirty town! I

shouldn't like that. Has your papa got a house here, then?'

'No, Ada; I live alone, or at least with another lady,' says Betha; 'but perhaps you have not heard that I am an actress. I have gone upon the stage.'

'*Upon the stage!*' repeat the sisters, with the becoming British horror of one of the noblest professions in the world; 'do you mean that you *act*, Betha—really *act, yourself!*' as if she could possibly act through anyone else.

'Yes; I act for money, in order that I may maintain myself,' replies Betha, firmly. ' I have left home, Ada, and I shall never live there again. I tell you this plainly, so that you may see the reason why I could not go and stay with you at Black Abbotts.'

'Nonsense! what difference does that make?' cries Ada, recovering from her first surprise. 'You are just the same that you always were, Betha (only much better looking), whatever you do; and I think it must be lovely to be an actress. You'll hardly believe it,' she adds, lowering her voice, 'but Ella and I have never been inside a theatre, not even at Christmas, papa's so horribly particular, you know, and mamma's afraid to go against him; but of course we've heard all about them, especially the pantomimes, and I have often thought how delicious it must feel to be a fairy with silver wings hanging in the air, only I suppose one would be a little giddy at first.'

'I don't know, I'm sure,' replies Betha, laughing; 'I've never been a fairy hanging in the air, Ada, so I cannot tell. But every-one is not of your opinion, and with your mamma and papa the fact of my being an actress will probably make a great difference.'

'I am sure it won't,' says Ada, confidently; 'and you'll see for yourself before long. And if mamma asks you to stay with us you will, won't you, Betha? and we will have such fun together!'

'Indeed, indeed I will! that is, if I can

get leave. I should enjoy it above everything !' cries the other girl, some of the
memories and feelings of her former life
coming back upon her with a rush, and
causing a fierce longing to go back to it
again, if only for a few short days.

CHAPTER XVII.

' DON'T TELL HER.'

THE Matthew girls get into their carriage and drive away gaily, kissing their hands to Betha until she is out of sight. Then Ella, leaning over from her position on the back seat, whispers in her sister's ear, so that the coachman cannot overhear them.

'Ada! ought you to have said what you did to Betha Durant? Do you think mamma will let her come, when she hears she is an actress?'

'Why not?' demands Ada, with a heightened colour, under the consciousness of a probable mistake; 'what do they do on the stage? Is it *wrong*, Ella?'

'Well, not exactly *wrong*, perhaps ; but I am sure it isn't thought *nice !* Miss Masters and mamma were talking about Lady Farley the other day, and why the county people don't visit her ; and Miss Masters said something about her having been an actress ; and mamma sent me out of the room, and I know it was just so that I might not listen.'

'I *hate* Miss Masters !' exclaims Ada, energetically ; ' she is a horrid ill-natured old maid, and if she hears anything about Betha being on the stage, she'll try and persuade mamma that we oughtn't to know her. I can't bear such spite. Our own schoolfellow, too—it would be too ridiculous ! Ella dear ! don't let us tell her.'

'What ! Miss Masters ! Of course not.'

'No—no ! mamma ! Betha doesn't call herself " Durant " on the stage : she said so just now, didn't she ? so, as we never go to the theatre, mamma will not be the wiser. I will undertake to make Betha ignore the subject, and we can pretend we know nothing about it.'

'But suppose it ever comes out, Ada! Won't mamma be awfully angry with us then?'

'We must say we didn't understand. How can we be expected to understand when papa never allows us to see the inside of a theatre. And I *do* want to have Betha at Black Abbotts, don't you, Ella?'

'Of course I do! I always liked her at college. She was so kind in helping me over those horrid themes and exercises. I would do a great deal for Betha Durant.'

'Then hold your tongue, my dear; that will be about as strong a proof of your affection as you could possibly give her; and let me manage the rest. She said she was staying with a friend at 15, Tavistock Gate. I shall repeat what she told us, and mamma shall write her an invitation to Black Abbotts and send it off by this evening's post.'

Who could withstand the combined strata-

gem of such a pair of manœuvrers? Evidently
not Mrs. Matthews, for when Betha comes
down to breakfast the following morning, a
letter lies on her plate, containing the most
cordial invitation to pass as long a time
as convenient to herself with her old school-
mates at Black Abbotts.

Notwithstanding the girls' assertions to the
contrary, she has hardly expected to receive
it, and the reception gives her the keenest
pleasure, accepting it (as she does) as a
proof that the profession she has adopted
need not necessarily shut her out from all
association with her former friends.

Miss Montalambert dare not quite take
upon herself the responsibility of telling
Betha to answer her invitation in the
affirmative (notwithstanding her assumed
authority in all her uncle's affairs), but she
talks as confidently of his consent to the
proposed plan, as if she had already obtained
it.

' My dear child !' she exclaims, ' you have

only to tell uncle you wish to go.   We don't
want you at present, you know ; and if we
should do so, we have only to send you a
telegram.   And it is the best thing possible
for you.   I'm sure I'm delighted your friends
should have thought of it.   It would kill me
to be out of the pantomime, as you are.
Quite a queer feeling comes over me sometimes in the middle of the evening lest you
should do something rash left here all by
yourself.   How you can stand it is a mystery ;
I'd rather be check-taker than out of the
fun.'

'I am never alone you know, Kate,'
replies Betha, smiling ; 'Mr. Cheyne gave
me a hint to under study "Medea" for the
spring, and she and I make a fine noise here
together, I can tell you, whilst you are
driving Messrs Ashton and Cook to mad-
ness.'

'Now, you naughty girl ! I won't be
laughed at.   Studying "Medea" are you,
and praying all the while that the celebrated

Miss Cuthbert, who is engaged for our "lead'
after the pantomime, may have a fit or a
stroke of paralysis, or something equally
nice to prevent her coming down to Buton.

'Why not put it in a milder form, Kate,
and say a husband or a coronet?' exclaims
Betha, laughing merrily. 'Fits and strokes
are such nasty ill-natured wishes. If Miss
Cuthbert's defection is to do me a good turn,
I would rather it came about in a pleasanter
way for her.'

'The question is, my dear, which *is* the
pleasanter way?' replies Miss Kate; 'I
allow a coronet *sounds* nice, but as it must
needs be linked with a *husband,* I am not
quite sure if one would not recover sooner
from the paralysis.'

Betha encounters no difficulty on the part
of the good-natured manager, who simply
desires her to hold herself in readiness to
return to duty on the first reception of a
telegram. So she writes a grateful little note
to Mrs. Matthews, accepting her invitation,

and expressing her willingness to go to Black
Abbotts at her hostess's earliest convenience.

And so on the very next day Ada and
Ella, delighted at the prospect of their
visitor, though somewhat dubious as to the
best method of binding her over to secrecy,
arrive in a high state of excitement, to bear
her away.

'Betha, dear,' says Ada, rather timidly,
as the carriage rolls rapidly with them to
Black Abbotts; 'will you mind my asking
you something?'

'How can I tell, Ada, before I hear it?'

'Well! it's nothing very out of the way,
only this: papa's an awful old fad, you know
—always praying and that sort of thing—now
don't look frightened. I must say one thing
for papa, he never forces other people to pray
too, whether they like it or not; but he's
dreadfully particular, and thinks everything
shocking; so don't talk of the theatre
before him or mamma, will you? there's a
dear.'

'But, Ada!' cries Betha, her sensitive nature immediately taking alarm. 'If your parents hold such sentiments, how can they approve of my visiting at Black Abbotts. Oh! I hope you and Ella haven't persuaded them to invite me against their better judgment.'

'Not a bit of it, Betha! What a funny girl you are. Of course mamma knows all about you, and that you are Major Durant's daughter, and is delighted that you should come to Black Abbotts—only, will you promise me not to say anything about the stage?—not before her or papa—because they don't like to talk of it—that's all.'

Still Betha's face looks troubled.

'I am afraid they are ashamed of me,' she says sadly.

'Not a bit of it!' cries Ada; 'only they like long prayers themselves better than theatres. Can't you understand? Why, even the people who only *go* to the play— like Miss Masters, and lots of others—never speak of what they have seen before papa, because he frowns and turns up the whites of his eyes until they are quite ill.'

'Oh, I see!' exclaims Betha; 'you don't want me to introduce the subject for fear of a lecture. Trust me, Ada! I like sermons as little as yourself. And, indeed, I have but little to tell. I have been for so short a time upon the stage, that it has been all drudgery as yet. And at no time should I much care, I think, to talk about myself. If the world never hears of my name, without my aid, the longer it remains in oblivion the better.'

'Well! that point's settled,' says Ada, blithely; 'and now we've got nothing to do but to enjoy ourselves.'

It appears likely they will do so. Black Abbotts is a beautiful old country seat, capable of affording every amusement to three lively girls, and Mrs. Matthews receives Betha with a motherly welcome that makes her feel quite at her ease. She and her husband, who were already middle-aged, when the double blessing was accorded them of twin daughters, look much too old to be the parents of Ada and Ella ; and *feel* much too old into the bargain.

Consequently, the young ladies rule the roast at Black Abbotts, and have done so from their infancy, so that the pious old father, especially, is generally but too glad to get out of their way and leave them to their own devices. No wonder, therefore, that they have so little scruple in hoodwinking their parents : and introducing their friend Miss Durant simply as an old schoolfellow, passing the winter in Buton with an acquaintance. And innocent Betha goes into the trap, blindfold, never doubting that she has been invited there, spite of her profession, and proportionately grateful for the fact.

The weeks pass rapidly away. One—two—three, have flown, and still the popularity of the Buton pantomime shows no signs of decrease, and Betha is left in peace to enjoy herself at Black Abbotts.

A hard frost sets in, and skating becomes the order of the day. The ornamental water in Mr. Matthews's park is frozen over, and the gates are thrown open for the benefit of the public.

'Now we shall have some real fun,' says Ada; 'papa is so horridly particular, you know, that he will not allow us to skate off the grounds, for fear of our being spoken to, or some rubbish of that sort; but he can hardly forbid our using our own ice, and there's been a right of way through the park for the last century, so he is unable to shut that up, either!'

' I am afraid your papa must find you and Ella rather careful blessings,' remarks Betha. ' I wonder what he would say if you showed an inclination to marry anybody!'

' I am sure I don't know! He'd have a fit, I suppose. You see, Betha, papa's a great deal too old for girls like us. He was seventy-six last birthday. How can you expect him to sympathise with the wishes and pursuits of eighteen? But he won't come down to the ice, thank goodness! It always makes him ill. And we shall have all the county people over here to-morrow, and no end of larks—everybody knows that Black Abbotts water makes the best skating in Somerset.'

On the following day, she is very busy pointing out the different visitors on the ice for Betha's edification.

'That's Lady Farley with the scarlet petticoat—the one that was *an actress*, you know,' she says in a whisper. 'Do you think her pretty? Miss Masters says she dyes her hair—but I don't know, I'm sure. I don't like it—it's just like a brass candle-stick—you'll never change the colour of *your* hair, will you, Betha? It would be ten thousand pities. And there's old Masters herself with her beaky nose and her piggy eyes! I can't bear that woman! I say all kinds of things to annoy her, and papa reads me lectures about "soft answers turning away wrath." Here comes Emily Stewart! She used to be at the Princess College with us, but she left before you came. Emily's awfully nice and clever; she wanted us once to join in some private theatricals at her mother's house—she said she was sure I could act, because I make such queer faces— and papa talked for three hours about the "devil's play-house," and the "bottomless pit," till we were all sick.'

'Oh, Ada! Ada! how wild you are!' cries Betha, 'I ought not to encourage your naughtiness, but I can't help laughing at it.'

'Of course you can't! I did not mean you to. But, Betha, skate down to the farthest corner of the pond with me, and I'll show you something really interesting—a rich young man!'

'Is a rich young man such a *rara avis* in Somerset, Ada?'

'Yes; they're scarce enough under any circumstances, but this young man is more than rich, he's eligible. He's an only son, and an only grandson, and his papa and his grandmamma are to leave him all their money, and they have made such an awful coddle of him that I wonder they let him out on the ice for fear he should take cold.

' And yet you call him interesting !'

'Of course he is, because he'll be so rich. To tell you the truth, Betha, I believe papa wants him to marry Ella or me, for he is always bringing him home to Black Abbotts unexpectedly to spend the evening with us. Papa's awfully pious, and always lecturing other people on their worldliness and love of gain, but he's got an eye to the main chance as well as his neighbours, I can tell you.'

' But *you* don't see it in the same light, Ada.'

' Not I, my dear. My fancy lies in quite a different direction. Now there's a young fellow called Grantham. Oh, Betha, he's

just divine! such eyes, such hair, and the
dearest, sweetest little silky moustache that
you ever saw—but no money of course.
Those handsome men never have, and papa
is always as surly with him as possible ; and
one evening, when he and I had slipped
away together into the conservatory to have
a little quiet talk, papa actually had the im-
pertinence to come after us, and he lectured
me so, and was so rude to Mr. Grantham
that he has never been near Black Abbotts
since. Wasn't it a horrid shame? I was in
such a rage with papa that I didn't speak to
him for three days afterwards. But now for
the interesting Robert! By the way, his
old grandame is to dine with us this evening.
Here comes his long nose down the left-hand
side. You might see it half a mile off without glasses. And with a comforter round
his throat, of course. The molly-coddle!
Stop, Betha! don't start yet. It's only fair
you should have a chance. Wait till I have
introduced him to you.'

Betha is laughing at the nonsense of her friend when a tall, lanky young man comes skating full tilt against them, and stretching out both his arms in an awkward endeavour to avoid the inevitable collision, nearly sends her flat upon her back.

CHAPTER XVIII.

'I NEVER THOUGHT TO MEET YOU HERE.'

'Now then, stupid!' cries the lively Ada, 'where are you going?'

The young man thus addressed makes a violent effort to regain his equilibrium, and then, with a very red face and breathing hard, he manages to get his hand to his hat, and commences to stammer out an apology. But the first words have barely left his lips before he interrupts them with an exclamation of surprise:

'Miss Durant! is it possible?'

'Oh, Mr. Frere! I never thought I should meet you down here!' and their hands are simultaneously extended to greet each other.

'Why, do you mean to say that you are already acquainted?' says Ada. 'What a little world this is! I declare I never prepare a pleasant surprise for my friends but I find they know all about it beforehand. Where on earth did you two meet?'

'In London, Miss Matthews. I have the honour to know Miss Durant's aunt, Mrs. Chapman, and we have met each other at her house frequently. But it is very strange that I should not have heard *you* mention Miss Durant's name, Miss Matthews, during the many evenings I have had the pleasure of spending at Black Abbotts.'

'Not at all, Mr. Frere. When gentlemen come to see *me*, I expect them to *think* of me and not of my friends, so I am careful not to introduce the subject. But really and truly, neither Ella nor I thought there was the remotest chance of getting dear Betha down here until we met her by mere accident in Buton.'

'Oh, are you staying in Buton? Is Mrs.

Chapman there, or—or any of your other friends ?'

Betha feels conscious as she answers :

' No, Mr. Frere, my aunt and cousin are still in London, and I have not been at Earl's Court since I left it to stay with Miss Kemyss at Albert Gate.'

' Were you there ? How vexatious ! I wish I had known it. I tried so hard to get your address from Miss Chapman, but she was so reserved on the subject that I became afraid that I had offended you beyond hope of pardon, and you had cautioned your aunt not to divulge your place of residence to me.'

This he ventures to say, seeing that Ada has skated a little way apart from them in order to recognise another friend. Betha grows scarlet, remembering the circumstances under which they parted, but her self-possession does not forsake her.

' Did we not part friends, Mr. Frere ?' she says quietly.

'We did, thanks to your goodness; and I trust we meet the same. Are you staying here for any time?'

'I am not sure. It is quite uncertain. I may be recalled any day.'

'Recalled to London?'

'No, to Buton, where I am living with a lady friend.'

'I hope you will not receive that summons, then, for a long time to come. How delightful it is to have met you! I suppose you know that my father's seat, Baron's Court, is only three miles from here!'

'Indeed, I know nothing. Ada has never mentioned your name, and this meeting was quite as great a surprise to me as to yourself.'

'Oh, you must come over and see the Court some day. It is such a fine old place, you will be charmed with it. I must speak to Mrs. Matthews about it this evening. By the way, we are all to dine at Black Abbotts to-night, and then I shall be able to introduce you to my grandmother, Lady Frere.'

'I am rather afraid of Lady Frere, from what I have heard of her,' says Betha, laughing nervously. 'Aunt Janie used to say she was so very rigid in her principles and notions of decorum.'

'But you won't think the worse of her for that, I am sure, Miss Durant,' replies Bobby, eagerly ; 'it is just what a lady should be. If my grandmother *has* a fault, it is pride of birth and an unstained name. The idea of a woman stepping out of her position to do anything that is lowering to herself or her family, is terrible to her. I think she is rather hard sometimes upon her own sex, and seems to forget that she was once young herself ; but she has been a kind and good grandmother to me ; a mother, I may say, for I do not remember my own.'

'She will never like *me !*' exclaims Betha, determinately.

'Don't say that ! Why shouldn't she ?'

' Because I am sure she won't—for a thousand things. In the first place, I am not at all her type of young lady. I am fearless, and independent, and love to have my own way.'

' But you will never do anything unbecoming a gentlewoman ! I will take my oath of that,' cries Bobby, hotly.

' Not in my own ideas of what is unbecoming. But many people might think my ideas all wrong. And Lady Frere is one.'

' Don't judge her before you have seen her,' says her companion, imploringly ; and then Ada returns to Betha's side, and the girls keep together for the remainder of the morning, and there is no opportunity for Bobby Frere to do more than let his eyes rest admiringly on Betha's figure whenever they are not diverted elsewhere. The homage is very unobtrusive, but it does not escape the notice of the Miss Matthews, who ' chaff' poor Betha unmercifully on the subject till dinner-time.

'You've made a conquest, my dear.
Hooray! Let me congratulate you! Mrs.
Robert Frere, of Baron's Court; and when
his old father's dead, you'll be Lady Frere,
with about fifteen thousand a year! Upon
my word, Ella, when I come to think of it,
ought we to sit down quietly and let her
carry off the prize? Why, the creature will
have enough to keep both of us, and as we
have made up our minds never to separate,
the arrangement will be most convenient.
Even his long nose will become a 'blessing
in disguise' (as papa says) under the circumstances. That will bear division as well
as his purse. Ella, my child! let us wear
our new blue dresses this evening and cut
this interloper out. Bobby will never be
able to withstand an assault from such combined forces.'

'You can easily cut me out,' says Betha,
laughing, 'for I have no dress to put on, Ada,
except the one I wear every evening. I
never thought you would have dinner-parties

at Black Abbotts, or I should have told you
that I was not prepared to do you credit!'

'My dear girl,' says Ada, 'there's a deep
plot underlying your apparent humility.
You know that your plain black dress is the
very thing to ingratiate you in the eyes of
Lady Frere. The old lady wears black velvet
and diamonds herself, but she considers that
young girls are much better without any
ornaments whatever. And, if Ella and I *do*
wear the blue dresses, she and papa will
retire to a corner, and shake their heads over
them for an hour together! No, no, you're
the girl for Bobby's grandmamma! I
shouldn't wonder if she ordered him to marry
you on the spot.'

'She might order a long time before I
should obey her,' says Betha, merrily, as the
girls separate to dress for dinner.

Lady Frere tallies well with Ada's description. As Betha enters the drawing-room
she finds herself led up to a grand dignified
old lady, clad in the richest black velvet.

Her features, though cast in a more refined mould, bear all the family characteristics, which she is so proud to see reproduced in her son and grandson.

Lady Frere's nose is long and sharp, her eyes brown and piercing, and the slender tapering fingers of her fine old hands are covered with the most magnificent diamond rings.

Her white hair, which is worn in two large puffed curls on either side her face, gives her the appearance of a Frenchwoman, which is enhanced by her wax-like complexion, and the perfect taste displayed in her attire.

She looks at Betha keenly as the girl courtesies gracefully before her.

'A daughter of Major Durant, did you say, Mrs. Matthews? Glad to know you, my dear! Glad to see you've got some one to teach you how to dress! It's very seldom I see a girl in a nice modest gown nowadays. They think of nothing but showing their shoulders and their feet. "When is a lady not a lady? When she's a little bear!" That's my favourite riddle—but very few girls can answer it as you could. And where does your father live ?—in London ?'

'Yes, Lady Frere.'

'He is a Durant of Morristown, I suppose. I knew one of the family some years ago. Willoughby,'—to her son—'you remember Sir Fergus Durant, who was staying in Rome with us in 'forty-three. He must be a connection of this young lady. All the Durants came from the same stock.'

Sir Willoughby Frere, who bears an almost ludicrous resemblance to his son, having the same height, features, colouring, and awkward gait, shambles forward and mutters some incoherent reply to his mother's question.

'Of course you do,' resumes the talkative old lady (if Bobby has any gifts of conversation, he has inherited them from his grandmother, and not from his father). 'No

one could forget Sir Fergus. He was a
delightful young man, and never missed any
of his religions duties. I hope you are re-
ligious, my dear! No good ever came of a
young woman that was not!'

'I—I—try to be so, madam,' replies
Betha, hesitatingly.

'You must do more than " *try*," my dear!
you must *be* so once and for all!' says Lady
Frere; 'and don't encourage too great a love
for dress, or flirting, or theatres, and such
vain amusements. They have been the
perdition of too many young people already.
If I thought our Robert set store on such
follies, it would break my heart.'

'Dinner is ready, Lady Frere,' says Mr.
Matthews, at this juncture, as he bears her
off upon his arm. Betha follows with Bobby.
The conversation she has just held depresses
her. If, with such sentiments, Lady Frere
knew of the calling she pursues, would she
condescend to sit down at the same table
with her. And has she the right to make

Mr. and Mrs. Matthews feel as uncomfortable as they must be feeling at the deception they are compelled to assist in keeping up ?

'*Do* you disapprove of theatres?' she whispers timidly to Bobby, as they file through the hall into the dining-room.

'I ? of course not! I think they're the jolliest things possible, and go to them whenever I have the opportunity. But I don't tell grandmamma. She is uncommonly particular—so, in fact, is my father. They consider theatres and all places of amusement *wrong!* Well, let them continue to think so. It pleases them, and it doesn't hurt us; and they'll never alter my opinion on the subject if they talk till Doomsday.'

'I am glad of that,' says Betha ; and she gives Bobby's arm a grateful little squeeze as she speaks. The young man misinterprets the action. She is glad—poor child—to think that there is one person, at least, who, if the truth were told, would not condemn her ; that she has one friend in the company

who she feels is not too good nor too pious
for her to talk to. The young people are
merry enough during the ensuing meal, and
Betha soon forgets the uneasiness caused by
Lady Frere's address. But as soon as the
ladies return to the drawing-room, she calls
the girl to her side again. She has taken a
fancy to her appearance. There is something
so refined and aristocratic-looking about the
cut of her features and the willowy lines of
her figure : something so true and good in
the earnest expression of her eye, and the
mobile curve of her pure sweet lips.

'You must come and see me at Baron's
Court, my dear,' she commences, 'I have
just asked Mrs. Matthews to bring you over.
We have a beautiful music-room there, and
a gallery of pictures and many other things,
that I think you would like to see.'

'You are very good, madam,' says Betha,
gratefully.

'And the loveliest lake all fringed with
evergreens !' interrupts Ada. 'Lady Frere,

does your ice bear well, and may we bring
our skates over and have a skate ?'

' Certainly, my dear, if your mamma approves of it. For my part, I don't think that
skating is a very desirable exercise for young
ladies. If they could pursue it by themselves, it might be different, but the presence
of gentlemen, and the love of display, and
the indelicate dresses now worn for the purpose, all tend to promote much folly. I hope
you do not wear those absurdly short dresses
on the ice, Miss Matthews. They are not
decent.'

' Oh no ! I always skate in a riding
habit !' cries Ada, mischievously.

' I need not put the question to you,'
continues Lady Frere, as her eyes rest ap-
provingly upon Betha.

' I do not possess a skating costume,' replies the girl, smiling ; ' so I am obliged to
appear in my ordinary dress.'

' All the better, my dear ; all the better,'
is the old lady's answer ; and she does not

even resent the marked attention shown by Bobby to Betha during the remainder of the evening.

The whole family, indeed, seem to have taken a fancy to the girl. Lady Frere insists upon fixing an early day for the visit to Baron's Court before she leaves, and Sir Willoughby, when shaking hands with Betha, intimates his pleasure at the prospect of welcoming her there, whilst Bobby, his face beaming with delight, stands by and shows his satisfaction by his blushes.

END OF VOL. I.

BILLING AND SONS, PRINTERS AND ELECTROTYPERS, GUILDFORD.